愛麗絲夢遊仙境

Alice's Adventures in Wonderland

原著雙語彩圖本

作者——路易士・卡洛爾（Lewis Carroll）

譯者——陳育堯

contents

Alice's Adventures in Wonderland

愛麗絲夢遊仙境

Alice's Adventures in Wonderland

All in the golden afternoon
Full leisurely we glide;
For both our oars, with little skill,
By little arms are plied,
While little hands make vain pretence
Our wanderings to guide.

Ah, cruel Three! In such an hour
Beneath such dreamy weather,
To beg a tale of breath too weak
To stir the tiniest feather!
Yet what can one poor voice avail
Against three tongues together?

Imperious Prima flashes forth
Her edict "to begin it"
In gentler tone Secunda hopes
"There will be nonsense in it!"
While Tertia interrupts the tale
Not more than once a minute.

Anon, to sudden silence won,
In fancy they pursue
The dream-child moving through a land
Of wonders wild and new,
In friendly chat with bird or beast
And half believe it true.

And ever, as the story drained
The wells of fancy dry,
And faintly strove that weary one
To put the subject by,
"The rest next time " "It is next time!"
The happy voices cry.

Thus grew the tale of Wonderland:
Thus slowly, one by one,
Its quaint events were hammered out
And now the tale is done,
And home we steer, a merry crew,
Beneath the setting sun.

Alice! A childish story take,
And with a gentle hand
Lay it where Childhood's dreams are twined
In Memory's mystic band,
Like pilgrim's wither'd wreath of flowers
Pluck'd in far-off land.

Chapter 1

Down the Rabbit-Hole

Alice was beginning to get very tired of sitting by her sister on the bank, and of having nothing to do: once or twice she had peeped into the book her sister was reading, but it had no pictures or conversations in it, "and what is the use of a book," thought Alice, "without pictures or conversation?"

So she was considering in her own mind (as well as she could, for the hot day made her feel very sleepy and stupid) whether the pleasure of making a daisy-chain would be worth the trouble of getting up and picking the daisies, when suddenly a White Rabbit with pink eyes ran close by her.

There was nothing so *very* remarkable in that; nor did Alice think it so *very* much out of the way to hear the Rabbit say to itself, "Oh dear! Oh dear! I shall be too late!" (when she thought it over afterwards, it occurred to her that she ought to have wondered at this, but at the time it all seemed quite natural); but when the Rabbit actually *took a watch out of its waistcoat-pocket*, and

looked at it, and then hurried on, Alice started to her feet, for it flashed across her mind that she had never before seen a rabbit with either a waistcoat-pocket, or a watch to take out of it, and burning with curiosity, she ran across the field after it, and fortunately was just in time to see it pop down a large rabbit-hole under the hedge.

In another moment down went Alice after it, never once considering how in the world she was to get out again.

The rabbit-hole went straight on like a tunnel for some way, and then dipped suddenly down, so suddenly that Alice had not a moment to think about stopping herself before she found herself falling down a very deep well.

Either the well was very deep, or she fell very slowly, for she had plenty of time as she went down to look about her, and to wonder what was going to happen next. First, she tried to look down and make out what she was coming to, but it was too dark to see anything; then she looked at the sides of the well, and noticed that they were filled with cupboards and bookshelves: here and there she saw maps and pictures hung upon pegs. She took down a jar from one of the shelves as she passed: it was labelled "*ORANGE MARMALADE*", but to her great disappointment it was empty; she did not like to drop the jar for fear of killing somebody, so managed to put it into one of the cupboards as she fell past it.

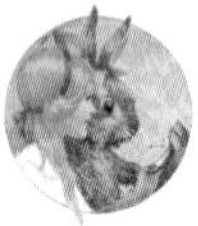

"Well!" thought Alice to herself. "After such a fall as this, I shall think nothing of tumbling downstairs! How brave they'll all think me at home! Why, I wouldn't say anything about it, even if I fell off the top of the house!" (Which was very likely true.)

Down, down, down. Would the fall *never* come to an end? "I wonder how many miles I've fallen by this time?" she said aloud. "I must be getting somewhere near the centre of the earth. Let me see: that would be four thousand miles down, I think—" (for, you see, Alice had learnt several things of this sort in her lessons in the schoolroom, and though this was not a *very* good opportunity for showing off her knowledge, as there was no one to listen to her, still it was good practice to say it over) "—yes, that's about the right distance—but then I wonder what Latitude or Longitude I've got to?" (Alice had no idea what Latitude was, or Longitude either, but thought they were nice grand words to say.)

Presently she began again. "I wonder if I shall fall right *through* the earth! How funny it'll seem to come out among the people that walk with their heads downwards! The Antipathies, I think—" (she was rather glad there *was* no one listening, this time, as it didn't sound at all the right word) "—but I shall have to ask them what the name of the country is, you know. Please, Ma'am, is this

New Zealand? Or Australia?" (and she tried to curtsey as she spoke—fancy *curtseying* as you're falling through the air! Do you think you could manage it?) "And what an ignorant little girl she'll think me! No, it'll never do to ask: perhaps I shall see it written up somewhere."

Down, down, down. There was nothing else to do, so Alice soon began talking again. "Dinah'll miss me very much tonight, I should think!" (Dinah was the cat.) "I hope they'll remember her saucer of milk at teatime. Dinah, my dear, I wish you were down here with me! There are no mice in the air, I'm afraid, but you might catch a bat, and that's very like a mouse, you know. But do cats eat bats, I wonder?" And here Alice began to get rather sleepy, and went on saying to herself, in a dreamy sort of way, "Do cats eat bats? Do cats eat bats?" and sometimes, "Do bats eat cats?" for, you see, as she couldn't answer either question, it didn't much matter which way she put it. She felt that she was dozing off, and had just

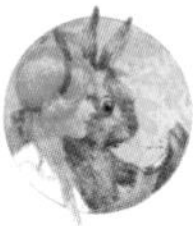

begun to dream that she was walking hand in hand with Dinah, and saying to her very earnestly, "Now, Dinah, tell me the truth: did you ever eat a bat?" when suddenly, thump! thump! down she came upon a heap of dry leaves, and the fall was over.

Alice was not a bit hurt, and she jumped up on to her feet in a moment: she looked up, but it was all dark overhead; before her was another long passage, and the White Rabbit was still in sight, hurrying down it. There was not a moment to be lost: away went Alice like the wind, and was just in time to hear it say, as it turned a corner, "Oh my ears and whiskers, how late it's getting!" She was close behind it when she turned the corner, but the Rabbit was no longer to be seen: she found herself in a long, low hall, which was lit up by a row of lamps hanging from the roof.

There were doors all round the hall, but they were all locked; and when Alice had been all the way down one side and up the other, trying every door, she walked sadly down the middle, wondering how she was ever to get out again.

Suddenly she came upon a little three-legged table, all made of solid glass; there was nothing on it except a tiny golden key, and Alice's first thought was that it might belong to one of the doors of the hall; but, alas! either the locks were too large, or the key was too small, but at any rate it would not open any of them. However, the second time round, she came upon a low curtain she had not noticed before, and behind it was a little door about fifteen inches high: she tried the little golden key in the lock, and to her great delight it fitted!

Alice opened the door and found that it led into a small passage, not much larger than a rat-hole: she knelt down and looked along the passage into the loveliest garden you ever saw. How she longed to get out of that dark hall, and wander about among those beds of bright flowers and those cool fountains, but she could not even get her

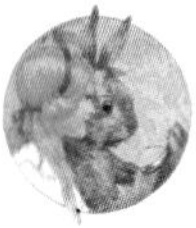

head through the doorway; "and even if my head would go through," thought poor Alice, "it would be of very little use without my shoulders. Oh, how I wish I could shut up like a telescope! I think I could, if I only know how to begin." For, you see, so many out-of-the-way things had happened lately, that Alice had begun to think that very few things indeed were really impossible.

There seemed to be no use in waiting by the little door, so she went back to the table, half hoping she might find another key on it, or at any rate a book of rules for shutting people up like telescopes: this time she found a little bottle on it ("which certainly was not here before," said Alice) and round its neck a paper label, with the words "DRINK ME" beautifully printed on it in large letters.

It was all very well to say "Drink me," but the wise little Alice was not going to do *that* in a hurry. "No, I'll look first," she said, "and see whether it's marked '*poison*' or not;" for she had read several nice little histories about children who had got burnt, and eaten up by wild beasts, and many other unpleasant things, all because they *would* not remember the simple rules their friends had taught them: such as, that a red-hot poker will burn you if you hold it too long; and that if you cut your finger *very* deeply with a knife, it usually bleeds; and she had never forgotten that if you drink much from a bottle marked "poison," it is almost certain to disagree with you, sooner or later.

However, this bottle was *not* marked "poison," so Alice ventured to taste it, and finding it very nice (it had, in fact, a sort of mixed flavour of cherry-tart, custard, pineapple, roast turkey, toffee, and hot buttered toast), she very soon finished it off.

"What a curious feeling!" said Alice. "I must be shutting up like a telescope."

And so it was indeed: she was now only ten inches high, and her face brightened up at the thought that she was now the right size for going though the little door into that lovely garden. First, however, she waited for a few minutes to see if she was going to shrink any further: she felt a little nervous about this; "for it might end, you know," said Alice, "in my going out altogether, like a candle. I wonder what I should be like then?" And she tried to fancy what the flame of a candle is like after it is blown out, for she could not remember ever having seen such a thing.

After a while, finding that nothing more happened, she decided on going into the garden at once; but, alas for poor Alice! when she got to the door, she found he had forgotten the little golden key, and when she went back to the table for it, she found she could not possibly reach it: she could see it quite plainly through the glass, and she tried her best to climb up one of the table-legs, but it was too slippery; and when she had tired herself out with trying, the poor little thing sat down and cried.

"Come, there's no use in crying like that!" said Alice to herself, rather sharply. "I advise you to leave off this minute!" She generally gave herself very good advice (though she very seldom followed it), and sometimes she scolded herself so severely as to bring tears into her eyes; and once she remembered trying to box her own ears for having cheated herself in a game of croquet she was playing against herself, for this curious child was very fond of pretending to be two people. "But it's no use now," thought poor Alice, "to pretend to be two people! Why, there's hardly enough of me left to make *one* respectable person!"

Soon her eye fell on a little glass box that was lying under the table: she opened it, and found in it a very small cake, on which the words "EAT ME" were beautifully marked in currants. "Well, I'll eat it," said Alice, "and if it makes me larger, I can reach the key; and if it makes me smaller, I can creep under the door; so either way I'll get into the garden, and I don't care which happens!"

She ate a little bit, and said anxiously to herself, "Which way? Which way?" holding her hand on the top of her head to feel which way it was growing, and she was quite surprised to find that she remained the same size: to be sure, this generally happens when one eats cake, but Alice had got so much into the way of expecting nothing but out-of-the-way things to happen, that it seemed quite dull and stupid for life to go on in the common way.

So she set to work, and very soon finished off the cake.

Chapter 2

The Pool of Tears

"Curiouser and curiouser!" cried Alice (she was so much surprised, that for the moment she quite forgot how to speak good English); "now I'm opening out like the largest telescope that ever was! Good-bye, feet!" (for when she looked down at her feet, they seemed to be almost out of sight, they were getting so far off). "Oh, my poor little feet, I wonder who will put on your shoes and stockings for you now, dears? I'm sure *I* shan't be able! I shall be a great deal too far off to trouble myself about you: you must manage the best way you can—but I must be kind to them," thought Alice, "or perhaps they won't walk the way I want to go! Let me see: I'll give them a new pair of boots every Christmas."

And she went on planning to herself how she would manage it. "They must go by the carrier," she thought; "and how funny it'll seem, sending presents to one's own feet! And how odd the directions will look!

Alice's Right Foot, Esq.,
Hearthrug,
Near The Fender
(with Alice's love).

Oh dear, what nonsense I'm talking!"

Just then her head struck against the roof of the hall: in fact she was now more than nine feet high, and she at once took up the little golden key and hurried off to the garden door.

Poor Alice! It was as much as she could do, lying down on one side, to look through into the garden with one eye; but to get through was more hopeless than ever: she sat down and began to cry again.

"You ought to be ashamed of yourself," said Alice, "a great girl like you" (she might well say this), "to go on crying in this way! Stop this moment, I tell you!" But she went on all the same, shedding gallons of tears, until there was a large pool all round her, about four inches deep and reaching half down the hall.

After a time she heard a little pattering of feet in the distance, and she hastily dried her eyes to see what was coming. It was the White Rabbit returning, splendidly dressed, with a pair of white kid gloves in one hand and a large fan in the other: he came trotting along in a

great hurry, muttering to himself as he came, "Oh! the Duchess, the Duchess! Oh! won't she be savage if I've kept her waiting!" Alice felt so desperate that she was ready to ask help of anyone; so, when the Rabbit came near her, she began, in a low, timid voice, "If you please, sir—" The Rabbit started violently, dropped the white kid gloves and the fan, and skurried away into the darkness as hard as he could go.

Alice took up the fan and gloves, and, as the hall was very hot, she kept fanning herself all the time she went on talking: "Dear, dear! How queer everything is today! And yesterday things went on just as usual. I wonder if I've been changed in the night? Let me think: was I the same when I got up this morning? I almost think I can remember feeling a little different. But if I'm not the same, the next question is, Who in the world am I? Ah, *that's* the great puzzle!" And she began thinking over all the children she knew that were of the same age as herself, to see if she could have been changed for any of them.

"I'm sure I'm not Ada," she said, "for her hair goes in such long ringlets, and mine doesn't go in ringlets at all;

and I'm sure I can't be Mabel, for I know all sorts of things, and she, oh! she knows such a very little! Besides, *she's* she, and *I'm* I, and—oh dear, how puzzling it all is! I'll try if I know all the things I used to know. Let me see: four times five is twelve, and four times six is thirteen, and four times seven is—oh dear! I shall never get to twenty at that rate! However, the Multiplication Table doesn't signify: let's try Geography. London is the capital of Paris, and Paris is the capital of Rome, and Rome—no, *that's* all wrong, I'm certain! I must have been changed for Mabel! I'll try and say '*How doth the little—*'" and she crossed her hands on her lap as if she were saying lessons, and began to repeat it, but her voice sounded hoarse and strange, and the words did not come the same as they used to do—

"How doth the little crocodile
Improve his shining tail,
And pour the waters of the Nile
On every golden scale!

How cheerfully he seems to grin,
How neatly spread his claws,
And welcomes little fishes in
With gently smiling jaws!"

"I'm sure those are not the right words," said poor Alice, and her eyes filled with tears again as she went on, "I must be Mabel after all, and I shall have to go and live in that poky little house, and have next to no toys to play with, and oh! ever so many lessons to learn! No, I've made up my mind about it; if I'm Mabel, I'll stay down here! It'll be no use their putting their heads down and saying 'Come up again, dear!' I shall only look up and say 'Who am I then? Tell me that first, and then, if I like being that person, I'll come up: if not, I'll stay down here till I'm somebody else'—but, oh dear!" cried Alice, with a sudden burst of tears, "I do wish they *would* put their heads down! I am so *very* tired of being all alone here!"

As she said this she looked down at her hands, and was surprised to see that she had put on one of the Rabbit's little white kid gloves while she was talking. "How *can* I have done that?" she thought. "I must be growing small again." She got up and went to the table to measure herself by it, and found that, as nearly as she could guess, she was

now about two feet high, and was going on shrinking rapidly: she soon found out that the cause of this was the fan she was holding, and she dropped it hastily, just in time to avoid shrinking away altogether.

"That *was* a narrow escape!" said Alice, a good deal frightened at the sudden change, but very glad to find herself still in existence; "and now for the garden!" and she ran with all speed back to the little door: but, alas! the little door was shut again, and the little golden key was lying on the glass table as before, "and things are worse than ever," thought the poor child, "for I never was so small as this before, never! And I declare it's too bad, that it is!"

As she said these words her foot slipped, and in another moment, splash! she was up to her chin in salt water. Her first idea was that she had somehow fallen into the sea, "and in that case I can go back by railway," she said to herself. (Alice had been to the seaside once in her life, and had come to the general conclusion that wherever you go to on the English coast you find a number of bathing machines in the sea, some children digging in the sand

with wooden spades, then a row of lodging houses, and behind them a railway station.) However, she soon made out that she was in the pool of tears which she had wept when she was nine feet high.

"I wish I hadn't cried so much!" said Alice, as she swam about, trying to find her way out. "I shall be punished for it now, I suppose, by being drowned in my own tears! That *will* be a queer thing, to be sure! However, everything is queer today."

Just then she heard something splashing about in the pool a little way off, and she swam nearer to make out what it was: at first she thought it must be a walrus or hippopotamus, but then she remembered how small she was now, and she soon made out that it was only a mouse that had slipped in like herself.

"Would it be of any use, now," thought Alice, "to speak to this mouse? Everything is so out-of-the-way down here that I should think very likely it can talk: at any rate, there's no harm in trying." So she began: "O Mouse, do you know the way out of this pool? I am very tired of swimming about here, O Mouse!" (Alice thought this must be the right way of speaking to a mouse: she had never done such a thing before, but she remembered having seen in her brother's Latin Grammar, "A mouse—of a mouse—to a mouse—a mouse—O mouse!") The Mouse looked at her rather inquisitively, and seemed to her to wink with one of its little eyes, but it said nothing.

"Perhaps it doesn't understand English," thought Alice; "I dare say it's a French mouse, come over with William the Conqueror." (For, with all her knowledge of history, Alice had no very clear notion how long ago anything had happened.) So she began again: "Où est ma chatte?" which was the first sentence in her French lesson-book. The Mouse gave a sudden leap out of the water, and seemed to quiver all over with fright. "Oh, I beg your pardon!" cried Alice hastily, afraid that she had hurt the poor animal's feelings. "I quite forgot you didn't like cats."

"Not like cats!" cried the Mouse, in a shrill, passionate voice. "Would *you* like cats if you were me?"

"Well, perhaps not," said Alice in a soothing tone: "don't

be angry about it. And yet I wish I could show you our cat Dinah: I think you'd take a fancy to cats if you could only see her. She is such a dear quiet thing," Alice went on, half to herself, as she swam lazily about in the pool, "and she sits purring so nicely by the fire, licking her paws and washing her face—and she is such a nice soft thing to nurse—and she's such a capital one for catching mice—oh, I beg your pardon!" cried Alice again, for this time the Mouse was bristling all over, and she felt certain it must be really offended. "We won't talk about her any more if you'd rather not."

"We, indeed!" cried the Mouse, who was trembling down to the end of his tail, "As if *I* would talk on such a subject! Our family always *hated* cats: nasty, low, vulgar things! Don't let me hear the name again!"

"I won't indeed!" said Alice, in a great hurry to change the subject of conversation. "Are you—are you fond—of—of dogs?" The Mouse did not answer, so Alice went on eagerly: "There is such a nice little dog near our house I should like to show you! A little bright-eyed terrier, you know, with oh, such long curly brown hair! And it'll fetch things when you throw them, and it'll sit up and beg for its dinner, and all sorts of things—I can't remember half of them—and it belongs to a farmer, you know, and he says it's so useful, it's worth a hundred pounds! He says it

kills all the rats and—oh dear!" cried Alice in a sorrowful tone, "I'm afraid I've offended it again!" For the Mouse was swimming away from her as hard as it could go, and making quite a commotion in the pool as it went.

So she called softly after it, "Mouse dear! Do come back again, and we won't talk about cats or dogs either, if you don't like them!" When the Mouse heard this, it turned round and swam slowly back to her: its face was quite pale (with passion, Alice thought), and it said in a low trembling voice, "Let us get to the shore, and then I'll tell you my history, and you'll understand why it is I hate cats and dogs."

It was high time to go, for the pool was getting quite crowded with the birds and animals that had fallen into it: there were a Duck and a Dodo, a Lory and an Eaglet, and several other curious creatures. Alice led the way, and the whole party swam to the shore.

Chapter 3

A Caucus-Race and a Long Tale

They were indeed a queer-looking party that assembled on the bank—the birds with draggled feathers, the animals with their fur clinging close to them, and all dripping wet, cross, and uncomfortable.

The first question of course was, how to get dry again: they had a consultation about this, and after a few minutes it seemed quite natural to Alice to find herself talking familiarly with them, as if she had known them all her life. Indeed, she had quite a long argument with the Lory, who at last turned sulky, and would only say, "I am older than you, and must know better;" and this Alice would not allow without knowing how old it was, and, as the Lory positively refused to tell its age, there was no more to be said.

At last the Mouse, who seemed to be a person of authority among them, called out, "Sit down, all of you, and listen to me! *I'll* soon make you dry enough!" They all sat down at once, in a large ring, with the Mouse in the middle. Alice kept her eyes anxiously fixed on it, for she felt sure she would catch a bad cold if she did not get dry very soon.

"Ahem!" said the Mouse with an important air, "Are you all ready? This is the driest thing I know. Silence all round, if you please! 'William the Conqueror, whose cause was favoured by the Pope, was soon submitted to by the English, who wanted leaders, and had been of late much accustomed to usurpation and conquest. Edwin and Morcar, the Earls of Mercia and Northumbria—'"

"Ugh!" said the Lory, with a shiver.

"I beg your pardon!" said the Mouse, frowning, but very politely: "Did you speak?"

"Not I!" said the Lory hastily.

"I thought you did," said the Mouse. "—I proceed. 'Edwin and Morcar, the Earls of Mercia and Northumbria, declared for him: and even Stigand, the patriotic Archbishop of Canterbury, found it advisable—'"

"Found *what*?" said the Duck.

"Found *it*," the Mouse replied rather crossly: "of course you know what 'it' means."

"I know what 'it' means well enough, when I find a thing," said the Duck: "it's generally a frog or a worm. The question is, what did the archbishop find?"

The Mouse did not notice this question, but hurriedly went on, " '—found it advisable to go with Edgar Atheling to meet William and offer him the crown. William's conduct at first was moderate. But the insolence of his Normans—" How are you getting on now, my dear?" it continued, turning to Alice as it spoke.

"As wet as ever," said Alice in a melancholy tone: "it doesn't seem to dry me at all."

"In that case," said the Dodo solemnly, rising to its feet, "I move that the meeting adjourn, for the immediate adoption of more energetic remedies—"

"Speak English!" said the Eaglet. "I don't know the meaning of half those long words, and, what's more, I don't believe you do either!" And the Eaglet bent down its head to hide a smile: some of the other birds tittered audibly.

"What I was going to say," said the Dodo in an offended tone, "was that the best thing to get us dry would be a Caucus-race."

"What *is* a Caucus-race?" said Alice; not that she much wanted to know, but the Dodo had paused as if it thought that *somebody* ought to speak, and no one else seemed inclined to say anything.

"Why," said the Dodo, "the best way to explain it is to do it." (And, as you might like to try the thing yourself some winter day, I will tell you how the Dodo managed it.)

First it marked out a racecourse, in a sort of circle ("the exact shape doesn't matter," it said), and then all the party were placed along the course, here and there. There was no "One, two, three, and away," but they began running when they liked, and left off when they liked, so that it was not easy to know when the race was over. However,

when they had been running half an hour or so, and were quite dry again, the Dodo suddenly called out, "The race is over!" and they all crowded round it, panting, and asking, "But who has won?"

This question the Dodo could not answer without a great deal of thought, and it sat for a long time with one finger pressed upon its forehead (the position in which you usually see Shakespeare, in the pictures of him), while the rest waited in silence. At last the Dodo said, "*Everybody* has won, and all must have prizes."

"But who is to give the prizes?" quite a chorus of voices asked.

"Why, *she*, of course," said the Dodo, pointing to Alice with one finger; and the whole party at once crowded round her, calling out in a confused way, "Prizes! Prizes!"

Alice had no idea what to do, and in despair she put her hand in her pocket, and pulled out a box of comfits (luckily the salt water had not got into it), and handed them round as prizes. There was exactly one a-piece all round.

"But she must have a prize herself, you know," said the Mouse.

"Of course," the Dodo replied very gravely. "What else have you got in your pocket?" he went on, turning to Alice.

"Only a thimble," said Alice sadly.

"Hand it over here," said the Dodo.

Then they all crowded round her once more, while the Dodo solemnly presented the thimble, saying, "We beg your acceptance of this elegant thimble;" and, when it had finished this short speech, they all cheered.

Alice thought the whole thing very absurd, but they all looked so grave that she did not dare to laugh; and, as she could not think of anything to say, she simply bowed, and took the thimble, looking as solemn as she could.

The next thing was to eat the comfits: this caused some noise and confusion, as the large birds complained that they could not taste theirs, and the small ones choked and had to be patted on the back. However, it was over at last, and they sat down again in a ring, and begged the Mouse to tell them something more.

"You promised to tell me your history, you know," said

Alice, "and why it is you hate—C and D," she added in a whisper, half afraid that it would be offended again.

"Mine is a long and a sad tale!" said the Mouse, turning to Alice and sighing.

"It is a long tail, certainly," said Alice, looking down with wonder at the Mouse's tail; "but why do you call it sad?" And she kept on puzzling about it while the Mouse was speaking, so that her idea of the tale was something like this—

"Fury said to a mouse, that he
met in the house, 'Let us
both go to law: I will
prosecute you.
Come, I'll take
no denial: we
must have a trial: for
really this morning
I've nothing to do.'
said the mouse
to the cur, 'Such
a trial, dear sir,
with no jury or judge,
would be wasting
our breath.' 'I'll be
judge, I'll be jury,'
said cunning
old Fury: 'I'll
try the whole
cause, and
condemn
you to
death."

"You are not attending!" said the Mouse to Alice severely. "What are you thinking of?"

"I beg your pardon," said Alice very humbly, "you had got to the fifth bend, I think?"

"I had *not*!" cried the Mouse, angrily.

"A knot!" said Alice, always ready to make herself useful, and looking anxiously about her. "Oh, do let me help to undo it!"

"I shall do nothing of the sort," said the Mouse, getting up and walking away . "You insult me by talking such nonsense!"

"I didn't mean it!" pleaded poor Alice. "But you're so easily offended, you know!"

The Mouse only growled in reply.

"Please come back and finish your story!" Alice called after it. And the others all joined in chorus, "Yes, please do!" but the Mouse only shook its head impatiently and walked a little quicker.

"What a pity it wouldn't stay!" sighed the Lory, as soon as it was quite out of sight; and an old Crab took the opportunity of saying to her daughter, "Ah, my dear! Let this be a lesson to you never to lose *your* temper!" "Hold your tongue, Ma!" said the young Crab, a little snappishly. "You're enough to try the patience of an oyster!"

"I wish I had our Dinah here, I know I do!" said Alice aloud, addressing nobody in particular. "She'd soon fetch it back!"

"And who is Dinah, if I might venture to ask the question?" said the Lory.

Alice replied eagerly, for she was always ready to talk about her pet: "Dinah's our cat. And she's such a capital one for catching mice you can't think! And oh, I wish you could see her after the birds! Why, she'll eat a little bird as soon as look at it!"

This speech caused a remarkable sensation among the party. Some of the birds hurried off at once: one old Magpie began wrapping itself up very carefully, remarking, "I really must be getting home; the night-air doesn't suit my throat!" and a Canary called out in a trembling voice to its children, "Come away, my dears! It's high time you were all in bed!" On various pretexts they all moved off, and Alice was soon left alone.

"I wish I hadn't mentioned Dinah!" she said to herself in a melancholy tone. "Nobody seems to like her, down here, and I'm sure she's the best cat in the world! Oh, my dear Dinah! I wonder if I shall ever see you any more!" And here poor Alice began to cry again, for she felt very lonely and low-spirited. In a little while, however, she again heard a little pattering of footsteps in the distance, and she looked up eagerly, half hoping that the Mouse had changed his mind, and was coming back to finish his story.

Chapter 4

The Rabbit Sends in a Little Bill

It was the White Rabbit, trotting slowly back again, and looking anxiously about as it went, as if it had lost something; and she heard it muttering to itself, "The Duchess! The Duchess! Oh my dear paws! Oh my fur and whiskers! She'll get me executed, as sure as ferrets are ferrets! Where *can* I have dropped them, I wonder?" Alice guessed in a moment that it was looking for the fan and the pair of white kid gloves, and she very good-naturedly began hunting about for them, but they were nowhere to be seen—everything seemed to have changed since her swim in the pool, and the great hall, with the glass table and the little door, had vanished completely.

Very soon the Rabbit noticed Alice, as she went hunting about, and called out to her in an angry tone, "Why, Mary Ann, what *are* you doing out here? Run home this moment, and fetch me a pair of gloves and a fan! Quick, now!" And Alice was so much frightened that she ran off at once in the direction it pointed to, without trying to explain the mistake it had made.

"He took me for his housemaid," she said to herself as she ran. "How surprised he'll be when he finds out who I am! But I'd better take him his fan and gloves—that is, if I can find them." As she said this, she came upon a neat little house, on the door of which was a bright brass plate with the name "W. RABBIT" engraved upon it. She went in without knocking, and hurried upstairs, in great fear lest she should meet the real Mary Ann, and be turned out of the house before she had found the fan and gloves.

"How queer it seems," Alice said to herself, "to be going messages for a rabbit! I suppose Dinah'll be sending me on messages next!" And she began fancying the sort of thing that would happen: " 'Miss Alice! Come here directly, and get ready for your walk!' 'Coming in a minute, nurse! But I've got to watch this mouse-hole till Dinah comes back, and see that the mouse doesn't get out.' Only I don't think," Alice went on, "that they'd let Dinah stop in the house if it began ordering people about like that!"

By this time she had found her way into a tidy little room with a table in the window, and on it (as she had hoped) a fan and two or three pairs of tiny white kid gloves: she took up the fan and a pair of the gloves, and was just going to leave the room, when her eye fell upon a little bottle that stood near the looking-glass. There was no label this time with the words "DRINK ME," but nevertheless she uncorked it and put it to her lips. "I know *something* interesting is sure to happen," she said to herself, "whenever I eat or drink anything; so I'll just see what this bottle does. I do hope it'll make me grow large again, for really I'm quite tired of being such a tiny little thing!"

It did so indeed, and much sooner than she had expected: before she had drunk half the bottle, she found her head pressing against the ceiling, and had to stoop to save her neck from being broken. She hastily put down the bottle, saying to herself, "That's quite enough—I hope I shan't grow any more—As it is, I can't get out at the door—I do wish I hadn't drunk quite so much!"

Alas! it was too late to wish that! She went on growing, and growing, and very soon had to kneel down on the floor: in another minute there was not even room for this, and she tried the effect of lying down with one elbow against the door, and the other arm curled round her head. Still she went on growing, and, as a last resource, she put one arm out of the window, and one foot up the chimney, and said to herself, "Now I can do no more, whatever happens. What *will* become of me?"

Luckily for Alice, the little magic bottle had now had its full effect, and she grew no larger: still it was very uncomfortable, and, as there seemed to be no sort of chance of her ever getting out of the room again, no

wonder she felt unhappy.

"It was much pleasanter at home," thought poor Alice, "when one wasn't always growing larger and smaller, and being ordered about by mice and rabbits. I almost wish I hadn't gone down that rabbit-hole—and yet—and yet—it's rather curious, you know, this sort of life! I do wonder what *can* have happened to me! When I used to read fairy-tales, I fancied that kind of thing never happened, and now here I am in the middle of one! There ought to be a book written about me, that there ought! And when I grow up, I'll write one—but I'm grown up now," she added in a sorrowful tone; "at least there's no room to grow up any more *here*."

"But then," thought Alice, "shall I *never* get any older than I am now? That'll be a comfort, one way—never to be an old woman—but then—always to have lessons to learn! Oh, I shouldn't like *that*!"

"Oh, you foolish Alice!" she answered herself. "How can you learn lessons in here? Why, there's hardly room for *you*, and no room at all for any lesson-books!"

And so she went on, taking first one side and then the other, and making quite a conversation of it altogether; but after a few minutes she heard a voice outside, and stopped to listen.

"Mary Ann! Mary Ann!" said the voice. "Fetch me my gloves this moment!" Then came a little pattering of feet on the stairs. Alice knew it was the Rabbit coming to look for her, and she trembled till she shook the house, quite forgetting that she was now about a thousand times as large as the Rabbit, and had no reason to be afraid of it.

Presently the Rabbit came up to the door, and tried to open it; but, as the door opened inwards, and Alice's elbow was pressed hard against it, that attempt proved a failure. Alice heard it say to itself, "Then I'll go round and get in at the window."

"*That* you won't" thought Alice, and, after waiting till she fancied she heard the Rabbit just under the window, she suddenly spread out her hand, and made a snatch in the air. She did not get hold of anything, but she heard a little shriek and a fall, and a crash of broken glass, from which she concluded that it was just possible it had fallen into a cucumber-frame, or something of the sort.

Next came an angry voice—the Rabbit's—"Pat! Pat! Where are you?" And then a voice she had never heard before, "Sure then I'm here! Digging for apples, yer honour!"

"Digging for apples, indeed!" said the Rabbit angrily. "Here! Come and help me out of *this*!" (Sounds of more broken glass.)

"Now tell me, Pat, what's that in the window?"

"Sure, it's an arm, yer honour!" (He pronounced it "arrum.")

"An arm, you goose! Who ever saw one that size? Why, it fills the whole window!"

"Sure, it does, yer honour: but it's an arm for all that."

"Well, it's got no business there, at any rate: go and take it away!"

There was a long silence after this, and Alice could only hear whispers now and then, such as: "Sure, I don't like it, yer honour, at all, at all!" "Do as I tell you, you coward!" and at last she spread out her hand again, and made another snatch in the air. This time there were *two* little shrieks, and more sounds of broken glass. "What a

number of cucumber-frames there must be!" thought Alice. "I wonder what they'll do next! As for pulling me out of the window, I only wish they *could*! I'm sure *I* don't want to stay in here any longer !"

She waited for some time without hearing anything more: at last came a rumbling of little cartwheels, and the sound of a good many voice all talking together; she made out the words: "Where's the other ladder?—Why I hadn't to bring but one; Bill's got the other—Bill! Fetch it here, lad!—Here, put 'em up at this corner—No, tie 'em together first—they don't reach half high enough yet—Oh! they'll do well enough; don't be particular— Here, Bill! catch hold of this rope—Will the roof bear!—Mind that loose slate—Oh, it's coming down! Heads below!" (a loud crash)—"Now, who did that?—it was Bill, I fancy—Who's to go down the chimney?—May, *I* shan't! *You* do it!—*That* I won't, then!—Bill's to go down—Here, Bill! the master says you've to go down the chimney!"

"Oh! So Bill's got to come down the chimney, has he?"

W-RABBIT

said Alice to herself. "Why, they seem to put everything upon Bill! I wouldn't be in Bill's place for a good deal: this fireplace is narrow, to be sure; but I *think* I can kick a little!"

She drew her foot as far down the chimney as she could, and waited till she heard a little animal (she couldn't guess of what sort it was) scratching and scrambling about in the chimney close above her: then, saying to herself, "This is Bill," she gave one sharp kick, and waited to see what would happen next.

The first thing she heard was a general chorus of, "There goes Bill!" then the Rabbit's voice along—"Catch him, you by the hedge!" then silence, and then another confusion of voices—"Hold up his head—Brandy now—Don't choke

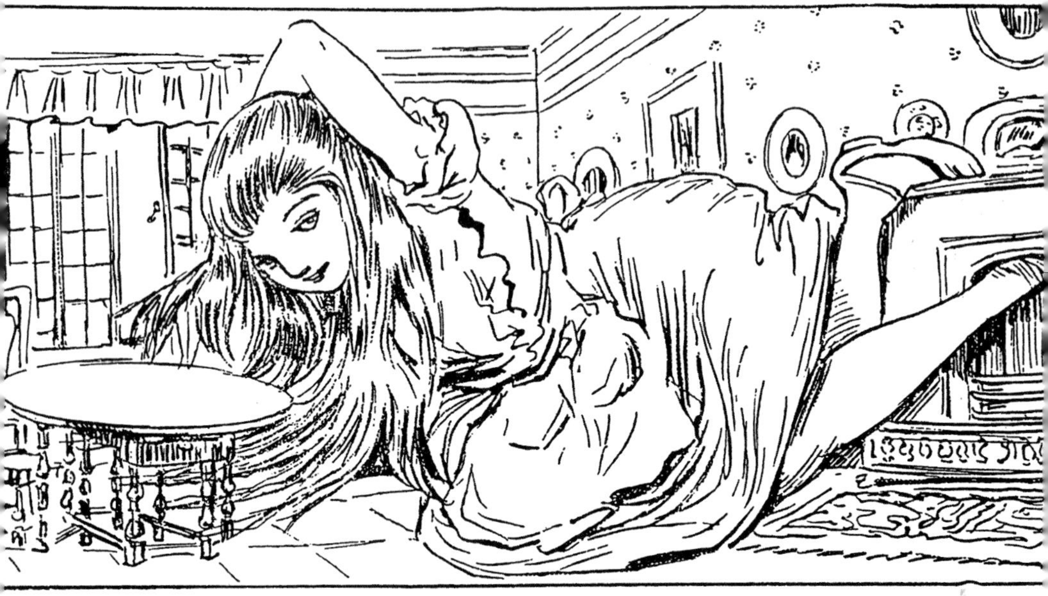

him—How was it, old fellow? What happened to you? Tell us all about it!"

At last came a little feeble, squeaking voice ("That's Bill," thought Alice), "Well, I hardly know—No more, thank ye; I'm better now—but I'm a deal too flustered to tell you—all I know is, something comes at me like a Jack-in-the-box, and up I goes like a sky-rocket!"

"So you did, old fellow!" said the others.

"We must burn the house down!" said the Rabbit's voice. And Alice called out as loud as she could, "If you do, I'll set Dinah at you!"

There was a dead silence instantly, and Alice thought to herself, "I wonder what they *will* do next! If they had any sense, they'd take the roof off." After a minute or two, they began moving about again, and Alice heard the Rabbit say, "A barrowful will do, to begin with."

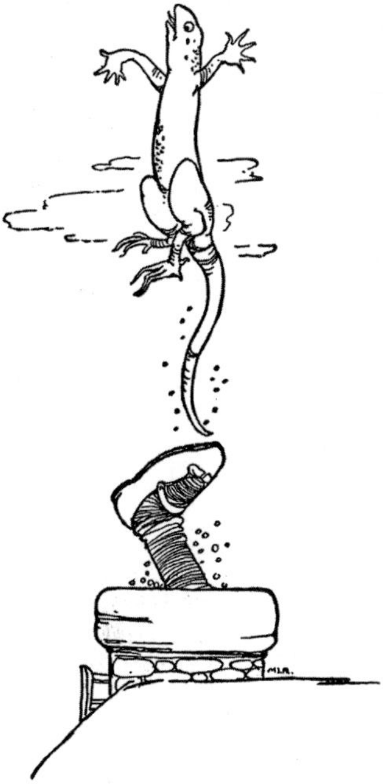

"A barrowful of *what*?" thought Alice. But she had not long to doubt, for the next moment a shower of little pebbles came rattling in at the window, and some of them hit her in the face. "I'll put a stop to this," she said to herself, and shouted out, "You'd better not do that again!" which produced another dead silence.

Alice noticed with some surprise that the pebbles were all turning into little cakes as they lay on the floor, and a bright idea came into her head. "If I eat one of these cakes," she thought, "it's sure to make *some* change in my size; and, as it can't possibly make me larger, it must make me smaller, I suppose."

So she swallowed one of the cakes, and was delighted to find that she began shrinking directly. As soon as she was small enough to get through the door, she ran out of the house, and found quite a crowd of little animals and birds waiting outside. The poor little Lizard, Bill, was in the middle, being held up by two guinea-pigs, who were giving it something out of a bottle. They all made a rush at Alice the moment she appeared; but she ran off as hard as she could, and soon found herself safe in a thick wood.

"The first thing I've got to do," said Alice to herself, as she wandered about in the wood, "is to grow to my right size again; and the second thing is to find my way into that lovely garden. I think that will be the best plan."

It sounded an excellent plan, no doubt, and very neatly and simply arranged; the only difficulty was that she had not the smallest idea how to set about it; and, while she was peering about anxiously among the trees, a little sharp bark just over her head made her look up in a great hurry.

An enormous puppy was looking down at her with large round eyes, and feebly stretching out one paw, trying to touch her. "Poor little thing!" said Alice, in a coaxing tone, and she tried hard to whistle to it; but she was terribly frightened all the time at the thought that it might be hungry, in which case it would be very likely to eat her up in spite of all her coaxing.

Hardly knowing what she did, she picked up a little bit of stick, and held it out to the puppy; whereupon the puppy jumped into the air off all its feet at once, with a yelp of delight, and rushed at the stick, and made believe to worry it; then Alice dodged behind a great thistle, to keep herself from being run over; and, the moment she appeared on the other side, the puppy made another rush

PEPPERMINT.

at the stick, and tumbled head over heels in its hurry to get hold of it; then Alice, thinking it was very like having a game of play with a cart-horse, and expecting every moment to be trampled under its feet, ran round the thistle again; then the puppy began a series of short charges at the stick, running a very little way forwards each time and a long way back, and barking hoarsely all the while, till at last it sat down a good way off, panting, with its tongue hanging out of its mouth, and its great eyes half shut.

This seemed to Alice a good opportunity for making her escape; so she set off at once, and ran till she was quite tired and out of breath, and till the puppy's bark sounded quite faint in the distance.

"And yet what a dear little puppy it was!" said Alice, as she leant against a buttercup to rest herself, and fanned herself with one of the leaves. "I should have liked teaching it tricks very much, if—if I'd only been the right size to do it! Oh dear! I'd nearly forgotten that I've got to grow up again! Let me see—how *is* it to be managed? I suppose I ought to eat or drink something or other; but the great question is, what?"

The great question certainly was, what? Alice looked all round her at the flowers and the blades of grass, but she could not see anything that looked like the right thing to

K M R

eat or drink under the circumstances. There was a large mushroom growing near her, about the same height as herself; and, when she had looked under it, and on both sides of it, and behind it, it occurred to her that she might as well look and see what was on the top of it.

She stretched herself up on tiptoe, and peeped over the edge of the mushroom, and her eyes immediately met those of a large blue caterpillar, that was sitting on the top with its arms folded, quietly smoking a long hookah, and taking not the smallest notice of her or of anything else.

Chapter 5

Advice from a Caterpillar

The Caterpillar and Alice looked at each other for some time in silence: at last the Caterpillar took the hookah out of its mouth, and addressed her in a languid, sleepy voice.

"Who are *you*?" said the Caterpillar.

This was not an encouraging opening for a conversation. Alice replied, rather shyly, "I—I hardly know, sir, just at present—at least I know who I *was* when I got up this morning, but I think I must have been changed several times since then."

"What do you mean by that?" said the Caterpillar sternly. "Explain yourself!"

"I can't explain *myself*, I'm afraid, sir," said Alice, "because I'm not myself, you see."

"I don't see," said the Caterpillar.

"I'm afraid I can't put it more clearly," Alice replied very politely, "for I can't understand it myself to begin with; and being so many different sizes in a day is very confusing."

"It isn't," said the Caterpillar.

"Well, perhaps you haven't found it so yet," said Alice; "but when you have to turn into a chrysalis—you will someday, you know—and then after that into a butterfly, I should think you'll feel it a little queer, won't you?"

"Not a bit," said the Caterpillar.

"Well, perhaps your feelings may be different," said Alice; "all I know is, it would feel very queer to *me*."

"You!" said the Caterpillar contemptuously. "Who are *you*?"

Which brought them back again to the beginning of the conversation. Alice felt a little irritated at the Caterpillar's making such very short remarks, and she drew herself up and said, very gravely, "I think you ought to tell me who *you* are, first."

"Why?" said the Caterpillar.

Here was another puzzling question; and as Alice could not think of any good reason, and as the Caterpillar seemed to be in a *very* unpleasant state of mind, she turned away.

"Come back!" the Caterpillar called after her. "I've something important to say!"

This sounded promising, certainly: Alice turned and came back again.

"Keep your temper," said the Caterpillar.

"Is that all?" said Alice, swallowing down her anger as well as she could.

"No," said the Caterpillar.

Alice thought she might as well wait, as she had nothing else to do, and perhaps after all it might tell her something worth hearing. For some minutes it puffed away without speaking, but at last it unfolded its arms, took the hookah out of its mouth again, and said, "So you think you're changed, do you?"

"I'm afraid I am, sir," said Alice; "I can't remember things as I used—and I don't keep the same size for ten minutes together!"

"Can't remember *what* things?" said the Caterpillar.

"Well, I've tried to say '*how doth the little busy bee*,' but it all came different!" Alice replied in a very melancholy voice.

"Repeat, '*You are old, Father William*,'" said the Caterpillar.

Alice folded her hands, and began—

"'You are old, Father William,' the young man said,
And your hair has become very white;
And yet you incessantly stand on your head—
Do you think, at your age, it is right?'

'In my youth,' Father William replied to his son.
'I feared it might injure the brain;
But, now that I'm perfectly sure I have none,
Why, I do it again and again.'

'You are old,' said the youth, 'as I mentioned before,
And have grown most uncommonly fat;
Yet you turned a back-somersault in at the door—
Pray, what is the reason of that?'

'In my youth,' said the sage, as he shook his grey locks,
'I kept all my limbs very supple
By the use of this ointment—one shilling the box—
Allow me to sell you a couple?'

"You are old," said the youth, "and your jaws are too weak
For anything tougher than suet;
Yet you finished the goose, with the bones and the beak—
Pray how did you manage to do it?"

'In my youth,' said his father, 'I took to the law,
And argued each case with my wife;
And the muscular strength, which it gave to my jaw,
Has lasted the rest of my life.'

'You are old,' said the youth, 'one would hardly suppose
That your eye was as steady as ever;
Yet you balanced an eel on the end of your nose—
What made you so awfully clever?'

'I have answered three questions, and that is enough,'
Said his father; 'don't give yourself airs!
Do you think I can listen all day to such stuff?
Be off, or I'll kick you downstairs!'"

"That is not said right," said the Caterpillar.

"Not *quite* right, I'm afraid," said Alice, timidly; "some of the words have got altered."

"It is wrong from beginning to end," said the Caterpillar decidedly, and there was silence for some minutes.

The Caterpillar was the first to speak.

"What size do you want to be?" it asked.

"Oh, I'm not particular as to size," Alice hastily replied; "only one doesn't like changing so often, you know."

"I *don't* know," said the Caterpillar.

Alice said nothing: she had never been so much contradicted in all her life before, and she felt that she was losing her temper.

"Are you content now?" said the Caterpillar.

"Well, I should like to be a *little* larger, sir, if you wouldn't mind," said Alice: "three inches is such a wretched height to be."

"It is a very good height indeed!" said the Caterpillar angrily, rearing itself upright as it spoke (it was exactly three inches high).

"But I'm not used to it!" pleaded poor Alice in a piteous tone. And she thought of herself, "I wish the creatures wouldn't be so easily offended!"

"You'll get used to it in time," said the Caterpillar; and it put the hookah into its mouth and began smoking again.

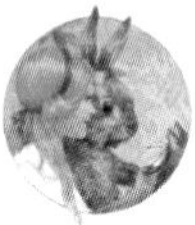

This time Alice waited patiently until it chose to speak again. In a minute or two the Caterpillar took the hookah out of its mouth and yawned once or twice, and shook itself. Then it got down off the mushroom, and crawled away into the grass, merely remarking as it went, "One side will make you grow taller, and the other side will make you grow shorter."

"One side of *what*? The other side of *what*?" thought Alice to herself.

"Of the mushroom," said the Caterpillar, just as if she had asked it aloud; and in another moment it was out of sight.

Alice remained looking thoughtfully at the mushroom for a minute, trying to make out which were the two sides of it; and as it was perfectly round, she found this a very difficult question. However, at last she stretched her arms round it as far as they would go, and broke off a bit of the edge with each hand.

"And now which is which?" she said to herself, and nibbled a little of the right-hand bit to try the effect: the next moment she felt a violent blow underneath her chin: it had struck her foot!

She was a good deal frightened by this very sudden change, but she felt that there was no time to be lost, as she was shrinking rapidly; so she set to work at once to eat some of the other bit. Her chin was pressed so closely against her foot that there was hardly room to open her mouth; but she did it at last, and managed to swallow a morsel of the left-hand bit.

"Come, my head's free at last!" said Alice in a tone of delight, which changed into alarm in another moment, when she found that her shoulders were nowhere to be found: all she could see, when she looked down, was an immense length of neck, which seemed to rise like a stalk out of a sea of green leaves that lay far below her.

"What *can* all that green stuff be?" said Alice. "And where *have* my shoulders got to? And oh, my poor hands, how is it I can't see you?" She was moving them about as she spoke, but no result seemed to follow, except a little shaking among the distant green leaves.

M.W.T.

As there seemed to be no chance of getting her hands up to her head, she tried to get her head down to them, and was delighted to find that her neck would bend about easily in any direction, like a serpent. She had just succeeded in curving it down into a graceful zigzag, and was going to dive in among the leaves, which she found to be nothing but the tops of the trees under which she had been wandering, when a sharp hiss made her draw back in a hurry: a large pigeon had flown into her face, and was beating her violently with its wings.

"Serpent!" screamed the Pigeon.

"I'm *not* a serpent!" said Alice indignantly. "Let me alone!"

"Serpent, I say again!" repeated the Pigeon, but in a more subdued tone, and added with a kind of sob, "I've tried every way, and nothing seems to suit them!"

"I haven't the least idea what you're talking about," said Alice.

"I've tried the roots of trees, and I've tried banks, and I've tried hedges," the Pigeon went on, without attending to her; "but those serpents! There's no pleasing them!"

Alice was more and more puzzled, but she thought there was no use in saying anything more till the Pigeon had finished.

"As if it wasn't trouble enough hatching the eggs," said

the Pigeon; “but I must be on the lookout for serpents night and day! Why, I haven’t had a wink of sleep these three weeks!”

“I’m very sorry you’ve been annoyed,” said Alice, who was beginning to see its meaning.

“And just as I’d taken the highest tree in the wood,” continued the Pigeon, raising its voice to a shriek, “and just as I was thinking I should be free of them at last, they must needs come wriggling down from the sky! Ugh, Serpent!”

“But I’m *not* a serpent, I tell you!” said Alice. “I’m a—I’m a—”

“Well! *What* are you?” said the Pigeon. “I can see you’re trying to invent something!”

“I—I’m a little girl,” said Alice, rather doubtfully, as she remembered the number of changes she had gone through, that day.

“A likely story indeed!” said the Pigeon in a tone of the deepest contempt. “I’ve seen a good many little girls in my time, but never *one* with such a neck as that! No, no! You’re a serpent; and there’s no use denying it. I suppose you’ll be telling me next that you never tasted an egg!”

“I *have* tasted eggs, certainly,” said Alice, who was a very truthful child; “but little girls eat eggs quite as much as serpents do, you know.”

"I don't believe it," said the Pigeon; "but if they do, why then they're a kind of serpent, that's all I can say."

This was such a new idea to Alice, that she was quite silent for a minute or two, which gave the Pigeon the opportunity of adding, "You're looking for eggs, I know *that* well enough; and what does it matter to me whether you're a little girl or a serpent?"

"It matters a good deal to *me*," said Alice hastily; "but I'm not looking for eggs, as it happens; and if I was, I shouldn't want *yours*: I don't like them raw."

"Well, be off, then!" said the Pigeon in a sulky tone, as it settled down again into its nest. Alice crouched down among the trees as well as she could, for her neck kept getting entangled among the branches, and every now and then she had to stop and untwist it. After a while she remembered that she still held the pieces of mushroom in her hands, and she set to work very carefully, nibbling first at one and then at the other, and growing sometimes taller and sometimes shorter, until she had succeeded in bringing herself down to her usual height.

It was so long since she had been anything near the right size, that it felt quite strange at first; but she got used to it in a few minutes, and began talking to herself, as usual. "Come, there's half my plan done now! How puzzling all these changes are! I'm never sure what I'm going to be from one minute to another! However, I've got back to my right size; the next thing is to get into that beautiful garden—how *is* that to be done, I wonder?" As she said this, she came suddenly upon an open place, with a little house in it about four feet high. "Whoever lives there," thought Alice, "it'll never do to come upon them *this* size: why, I should frighten them out of their wits!" So she began nibbling at the right-hand bit again, and did not venture to go near the house till she had brought herself down to nine inches high.

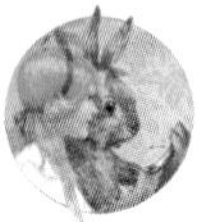

Chapter 6

Pig and Pepper

For a minute or two she stood looking at the house, and wondering what to do next, when suddenly a footman in livery came running out of the wood—(she considered him to be a footman because he was in livery: otherwise, judging by his face only, she would have called him a fish)—and rapped loudly at the door with his knuckles. It was opened by another footman in livery, with a round face and large eyes like a frog; and both footmen, Alice noticed, had powdered hair that curled all over their heads. She felt very curious to know what it was all about, and crept a little way out of the wood to listen.

The Fish-Footman began by producing from under his arm a great letter, nearly as large as himself, and this he handed over to the other, saying, in a solemn tone, "For the Duchess. An invitation from the Queen to play croquet." The Frog-Footman repeat-ed, in the same solemn tone, only changing the order of the words a little, "From the Queen. An invitation for the Duchess to play croquet."

Then they both bowed low, and their curls got entangled together.

Alice laughed so much at this, that she had to run back into the wood for fear of their hearing her; and, when she next peeped out the Fish-Footman was gone, and the other was sitting on the ground near the door, staring stupidly up into the sky.

Alice went timidly up to the door, and knocked.

"There's no sort of use in knocking," said the Footman, "and that for two reasons. First, because I'm on the same side of the door as you are; secondly, because they're making such a noise inside, no one could possibly hear you." And certainly there was a most extraordinary noise going on within—a constant howling and sneezing, and every now and then a great crash, as if a dish or kettle had been broken to pieces.

"Please, then," said Alice, "how am I to get in?"

"There might be some sense in your knocking," the Footman went on without attending to her, "if we had the door between us. For instance, if you were *inside*, you might knock, and I could let you out, you know." He was

looking up into the sky all the time he was speaking, and this Alice thought decidedly uncivil. "But perhaps he can't help it," she said to herself; "his eyes are so *very* nearly at the top of his head. But at any rate he might answer questions.—How am I to get in?" she repeated, aloud.

"I shall sit here," the Footman remarked, "till tomorrow—"

At this moment the door of the house opened, and a large plate came skimming out, straight at the Footman's head: it just grazed his nose, and broke to pieces against one of the trees behind him.

"—or next day, maybe," the Footman continued in the same tone, exactly as if nothing had happened.

"How am I to get in?" asked Alice again, in a louder tone.

"*Are* you to get in at all?" said the Footman. "That's the first question, you know."

It was, no doubt: only Alice did not like to be told so. "It's really dreadful," she muttered to herself, "the way all the creatures argue. It's enough to drive one crazy!"

The Footman seemed to think this a good opportunity for repeating his remark, with variations. "I shall sit here," he said, "on and off, for days and days."

"But what am *I* to do?" said Alice.

"Anything you like," said the Footman, and began whistling.

"Oh, there's no use in talking to him," said Alice desperately: "he's perfectly idiotic!" And she opened the door and went in.

The door led right into a large kitchen, which was full of smoke from one end to the other: the Duchess was sitting on a three-legged stool in the middle, nursing a baby; the cook was leaning over the fire, stirring a large cauldron which seemed to be full of soup.

"There's certainly too much pepper in that soup!" Alice said to herself, as well as she could for sneezing.

There was certainly too much of it in the *air*. Even the Duchess sneezed occasionally; and the baby was sneezing and howling alternately without a moment's pause. The only things in the kitchen that did not sneeze were the cook and a large cat which was sitting on the hearth and grinning from ear to ear.

"Please would you tell me," said Alice a little timidly, for she was not quite sure whether it was good manners for her to speak first, "why your cat grins like that?"

"It's a Cheshire cat," said the Duchess, "and that's why. Pig!"

She said the last word with such sudden violence that Alice quite jumped; but she saw in another moment that it was addressed to the baby, and not to her, so she took courage, and went on again—

"I didn't know that Cheshire cats always grinned; in fact, I didn't know that cats *could* grin."

"They all can," said the Duchess; "and most of 'em do."

"I don't know of any that do," Alice said very politely, feeling quite pleased to have got into a conversation.

"You don't know much," said the Duchess; "and that's a fact."

Alice did not at all like the tone of this remark, and thought it would be as well to introduce some other subject of conversation. While she was trying to fix on one, the cook took the cauldron of soup off the fire, and at once set to work throwing everything within her reach at the Duchess and the baby—the fire-irons came first; then followed a shower of saucepans, plates, and dishes. The Duchess took no notice of them even when they hit her;

Arthur Rackham

and the baby was howling so much already that it was quite impossible to say whether the blows hurt it or not.

"Oh, *please* mind what you're doing!" cried Alice, jumping up and down in an agony of terror. "Oh, there goes his *precious* nose!" as an unusually large saucepan flew close by it, and very nearly carried it off.

"If everybody minded their own business," the Duchess said in a hoarse growl, "the world would go round a deal faster than it does."

"Which would *not* be an advantage," said Alice, who felt very glad to get an opportunity of showing off a little of her knowledge. "Just think of what work it would make with the day and night! You see the earth takes twenty-four hours to turn round on its axis—"

"Talking of axes," said the Duchess, "chop off her head!"

Alice glanced rather anxiously at the cook, to see if she meant to take the hint; but the cook was busily engaged in stirring the soup, and did not seemed not to be listening, so she ventured to go on again: "Twenty-four hours, I *think*; or is it twelve? I—"

"Oh, don't bother *me*," said the Duchess; "I never could abide figures!" And with that she began nursing her child again, singing a sort of lullaby to it as she did so, and giving it a violent shake at the end of every line:

"Speak roughly to your little boy,
And beat him when he sneezes:
He only does it to annoy,
Because he knows it teases."

CHORUS.
(In which the cook and the baby joined)—
"Wow! wow! wow!"

While the Duchess sang the second verse of the song, she kept tossing the baby violently up and down, and the poor little thing howled so, that Alice could hardly hear the words—

"I speak severely to my boy,
I beat him when he sneezes;
For he can thoroughly enjoy
The pepper when he pleases!"

CHORUS.
"Wow! wow! wow!"

"Here! you may nurse it a bit, if you like!" the Duchess said to Alice, flinging the baby at her as she spoke. "I must go and get ready to play croquet with the Queen," and

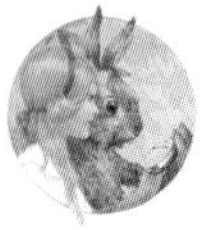

she hurried out of the room. The cook threw a frying-pan after her as she went out, but it just missed her.

Alice caught the baby with some difficulty as it was a queer-shaped little creature, and held out its arms and legs in all directions, "just like a starfish," thought Alice. The poor little thing was snorting like a steam-engine when she caught it, and kept doubling itself up and straightening itself out again, so that altogether, for the first minute or two, it was as much as she could do to hold it.

As soon as she had made out the proper way of nursing it (which was to twist it up into a sort of knot, and then keep tight hold of its right ear and left foot, so as to prevent its undoing itself), she carried it out into the open air. "If I don't take this child away with me," thought Alice, "they're sure to kill it in a day or two: wouldn't it be murder to leave it behind?" She said the last words out loud, and the little thing grunted in reply (it had left off sneezing by this time). "Don't grunt," said Alice; "that's not at all a proper way of expressing yourself."

The baby grunted again, and Alice looked very anxiously into its face to see what was the matter with it. There could be no doubt that it had a *very* turn-up nose, much more like a snout than a real nose; also its eyes were getting extremely small for a baby: altogether Alice did not like the look of the thing at all. "But perhaps it was

only sobbing," she thought, and looked into its eyes again, to see if there were any tears.

No, there were no tears. "If you're going to turn into a pig, my dear," said Alice, seriously, "I'll have nothing more to do with you. Mind now!" The poor little thing sobbed again (or grunted, it was impossible to say which), and they went on for some while in silence.

Alice was just beginning to think to herself, "Now, what am I to do with this creature when I get it home?" when it grunted again, so violently, that she looked down into its face in some alarm. This time there could be *no* mistake about it: it was neither more nor less than a pig, and she felt that it would be quite absurd for her to carry it any further.

So she set the little creature down, and felt quite relieved to see it trot away quietly into the wood. "If it had grown up," she said to herself, "it would have made a dreadfully ugly child: but it makes rather a handsome pig, I think." And she began thinking over other children she knew, who might do very well as pigs, and was just saying to herself, "if one only knew the right way to change them—" when she was a little startled by seeing the Cheshire Cat sitting on a bough of a tree a few yards off.

The Cat only grinned when it saw Alice. It looked good-natured, she thought: still it had *very* long claws and a great many teeth, so she felt that it ought to be treated with respect.

"Cheshire Puss," she began, rather timidly, as she did not at all know whether it would like the name: however, it only grinned a little wider. "Come, it's pleased so far," thought Alice, and she went on. "Would you tell me, please, which way I ought to go from here?"

"That depends a good deal on where you want to get to," said the Cat.

"I don't much care where—" said Alice.

"Then it doesn't matter which way you go," said the Cat.

"—so long as I get *somewhere*," Alice added as an explanation.

"Oh, you're sure to do that," said the Cat, "if you only walk long enough."

Alice felt that this could not be denied, so she tried another question. "What sort of people live about here?"

"In *that* direction," the Cat said, waving its right paw round, "lives a Hatter: and in *that* direction," waving the other paw, "lives a March Hare. Visit either you like: they're both mad."

"But I don't want to go among mad people," Alice remarked.

"Oh, you can't help that," said the Cat: "we're all mad here. I'm mad. You're mad."

"How do you know I'm mad?" said Alice.

"You must be," said the Cat, "or you wouldn't have come here."

Alice didn't think that proved it at all; however, she went on. "And how do you know that you're mad?"

"To begin with," said the Cat, "a dog's not mad. You grant that?"

"I suppose so," said Alice.

"Well, then," the Cat went on, "you see a dog growls when it's angry, and wags its tail when it's pleased. Now *I* growl when I'm pleased, and wag my tail when I'm angry. Therefore I'm mad."

"*I* call it purring, not growling," said Alice.

"Call it what you like," said the Cat. "Do you play croquet with the Queen today?"

"I should like it very much," said Alice, "but I haven't been invited yet."

"You'll see me there," said the Cat, and vanished.

Alice was not much surprised at this, she was getting so used to queer things happening. While she was looking at the place where it had been, it suddenly appeared again.

"By the by, what became of the baby?" said the Cat. "I'd nearly forgotten to ask."

"It turned into a pig," Alice answered very quietly, just as if it had come back in a natural way.

"I thought it would," said the Cat, and vanished again.

Alice waited a little, half expecting to see it again, but it did not appear, and after a minute or two she walked on in the direction in which the March Hare was said to live. "I've seen hatters before," she said to herself; "the March Hare will be much the most interesting, and perhaps, as this is May, it won't be raving mad—at least not so mad as it was in March." As she said this, she looked up, and there was the Cat again, sitting on a branch of a tree.

"Did you say pig, or fig?" said the Cat.

"I said pig," replied Alice; "and I wish you wouldn't keep appearing and vanishing so suddenly: you make one quite giddy."

"All right," said the Cat; and this time it vanished quite slowly, beginning with the end of the tail, and ending with the grin, which remained some time after the rest of it had gone.

"Well! I've often seen a cat without a grin," thought Alice; "but a grin without a cat! It's the most curious thing I ever saw in my life!"

She had not gone much farther before she came in sight of the house of the March Hare: she thought it must be the right house, because the chimneys were shaped like ears and the roof was thatched with fur. It was so large a house, that she did not like to go nearer till she had nibbled some more of the left-hand bit of mushroom, and raised herself to about two feet high: even then she walked up towards it rather timidly, saying to herself, "Suppose it should be raving mad after all! I almost wish I'd gone to see the Hatter instead!"

10/6

Chapter 7

A Mad Tea-Party

There was a table set out under a tree in front of the house, and the March Hare and the Hatter were having tea at it: a Dormouse was sitting between them, fast asleep, and the other two were resting their elbows on it, and talking over its head. "Very uncomfortable for the Dormouse," thought Alice; "only, as it's asleep, I suppose it doesn't mind."

The table was a large one, but the three were all crowded together at one corner of it. "No room! No room!" they cried out when they saw Alice coming. "There's *plenty* of room!" said Alice indignantly, and she sat down in a large armchair at one end of the table.

"Have some wine," the March Hare said in an encouraging tone.

Alice looked all round the table, but there was nothing on it but tea. "I don't see any wine," she remarked.

"There isn't any," said the March Hare.

"Then it wasn't very civil of you to offer it," said Alice angrily.

"It wasn't very civil of you to sit down without being

invited," said the March Hare.

"I didn't know it was *your* table," said Alice; "it's laid for a great many more than three."

"Your hair wants cutting," said the Hatter. He had been looking at Alice for some time with great curiosity, and this was his first speech.

"You shouldn't make personal remarks," Alice said with some severity; "it's very rude."

The Hatter opened his eyes very wide on hearing this; but all he *said* was, "Why is a raven like a writing-desk?"

"Come, we shall have some fun now!" thought Alice. "I'm glad they've begun asking riddles—I believe I can guess that," she added aloud.

"Do you mean that you think you can find out the answer to it?" said the March Hare.

"Exactly so," said Alice.

"Then you should say what you mean," the March Hare went on.

"I do," Alice hastily replied; "at least—at least I mean what I say—that's the same thing, you know."

"Not the same thing a bit!" said the Hatter. "You might just as well say that 'I see what I eat' is the same thing as 'I eat what I see!'"

"You might just as well say," added the March Hare, "that 'I like what I get' is the same thing as 'I get what I like!'"

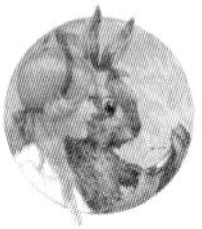

"You might just as well say," added the Dormouse, who seemed to be talking in his sleep, "that 'I breathe when I sleep' is the same thing as 'I sleep when I breathe!'"

"It *is* the same thing with you," said the Hatter, and here the conversation dropped, and the party sat silent for a minute, while Alice thought over all she could remember about ravens and writing-desks, which wasn't much.

The Hatter was the first to break the silence. "What day of the month is it?" he said, turning to Alice: he had taken his watch out of his pocket, and was looking at it uneasily, shaking it every now and then, and holding it to his ear.

Alice considered a little, and then said, "The fourth."

"Two days wrong!" sighed the Hatter. "I told you butter wouldn't suit the works!" he added, looking angrily at the March Hare.

"It was the *best* butter," the March Hare meekly replied.

"Yes, but some crumbs must have got in as well," the Hatter grumbled; "you shouldn't have put it in with the breadknife."

The March Hare took the watch and looked at it gloomily: then he dipped it into his cup of tea, and looked at it again: but he could think of nothing better to say than his first remark, "It was the *best* butter, you know."

Alice had been looking over his shoulder with some curiosity. "What a funny watch!" she remarked. "It tells the day of the month and doesn't tell what o'clock it is!"

"Why should it?" muttered the Hatter. "Does *your* watch tell you what year it is?"

"Of course not," Alice replied very readily: "but that's because it stays the same year for such a long time together."

"Which is just the case with *mine*," said the Hatter.

Alice felt dreadfully puzzled. The Hatter's remark seemed to have no meaning in it, and yet it was certainly English. "I don't quite understand," she said, as politely as she could.

"The Dormouse is asleep again," said the Hatter, and he poured a little hot tea upon its nose.

The Dormouse shook its head impatiently, and said, without opening its eyes, "Of course, of course; just what I was going to remark myself."

"Have you guessed the riddle yet?" the Hatter said, turning to Alice again.

"No, I give it up," Alice replied: "what's the answer?"

"I haven't the slightest idea," said the Hatter.

"Nor I," said the March Hare.

Alice sighed wearily. "I think you might do something better with the time," she said, "than waste it asking riddles with no answers."

"If you knew Time as well as I do," said the Hatter, "you wouldn't talk about wasting *it*. It's *him*."

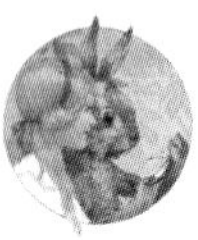

"I don't know what you mean," said Alice.

"Of course you don't!" the Hatter said, tossing his head contemptuously. "I dare say you never even spoke to Time!"

"Perhaps not," Alice cautiously replied: "but I know I have to beat time when I learn music."

"Ah! that accounts for it," said the Hatter. "He won't stand beating. Now, if you only kept on good terms with him, he'd do almost anything you liked with the clock. For instance, suppose it were nine o'clock in the morning, just time to begin lessons: you'd only have to whisper a hint to Time, and round goes the clock in a twinkling! Half-past one, time for dinner!"

("I only wish it was," the March Hare said to itself in a whisper.)

"That would be grand, certainly," said Alice thoughtfully: "but then—I shouldn't be hungry for it, you know."

"Not at first, perhaps," said the Hatter: "but you could keep it to half-past one as long as you liked."

"Is that the way *you* manage?" Alice asked.

The Hatter shook his head mournfully. "Not I!" he replied. "We quarrelled last March—just before *he* went mad, you know—" (pointing with his teaspoon at the March Hare) "—it was at the great concert given by the Queen of Hearts, and I had to sing—

In this Style
10/6
Pu

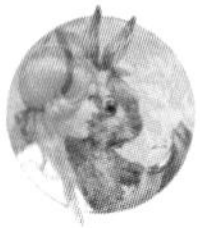

Twinkle, twinkle, little bat!
How I wonder what you're at!

You know the song, perhaps?"

"I've heard something like it," said Alice.

"It goes on, you know," the Hatter continued, "in this way —

Up above the world you fly,
Like a tea-tray in the sky.
Twinkle, twinkle —

Here the Dormouse shook itself, and began singing in its sleep, "*Twinkle, twinkle, twinkle, twinkle—*" and went on so long that they had to pinch it to make it stop.

"Well, I'd hardly finished the first verse," said the Hatter, "when the Queen jumped up and bawled out, 'He's murdering the time! Off with his head!'"

"How dreadfully savage!" exclaimed Alice.

"And ever since that," the Hatter went on in a mournful tone, "he won't do a thing I ask! It's always six o'clock now."

A bright idea came into Alice's head. "Is that the reason so many tea-things are put out here?" she asked.

"Yes, that's it," said the Hatter with a sigh: "it's always

teatime, and we've no time to wash the things between whiles."

"Then you keep moving round, I suppose?" said Alice.

"Exactly so," said the Hatter: "as the things get used up."

"But what happens when you come to the beginning again?" Alice ventured to ask.

"Suppose we change the subject," the March Hare interrupted, yawning. "I'm getting tired of this. I vote the young lady tells us a story."

"I'm afraid I don't know one," said Alice, rather alarmed at the proposal.

"Then the Dormouse shall!" they both cried. "Wake up, Dormouse!" And they pinched it on both sides at once.

The Dormouse slowly opened his eyes. "I wasn't asleep," he said in a hoarse, feeble voice: "I heard every word you fellows were saying."

"Tell us a story!" said the March Hare.

"Yes, please do!" pleaded Alice.

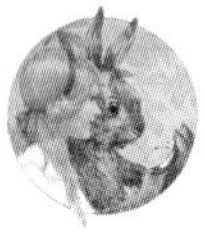

"And be quick about it," added the Hatter, "or you'll be asleep again before it's done."

"Once upon a time there were three little sisters," the Dormouse began in a great hurry; "and their names were Elsie, Lacie and Tillie; and they lived at the bottom of a well—"

"What did they live on?" said Alice, who always took a great interest in questions of eating and drinking.

"They lived on treacle," said the Dormouse, after thinking a minute or two.

"They couldn't have done that, you know," Alice gently remarked; "they'd have been ill."

"So they were," said the Dormouse; "*very* ill."

Alice tried to fancy to herself what such an extraordinary ways of living would be like, but it puzzled her too much, so she went on: "But why did they live at the bottom of a well?"

"Take some more tea," the March Hare said to Alice, very earnestly.

"I've had nothing yet," Alice replied in an offended tone, "so I can't take more."

"You mean you can't take *less*," said the Hatter: "it's very easy to take *more* than nothing."

"Nobody asked *your* opinion," said Alice.

"Who's making personal remarks now?" the Hatter asked triumphantly.

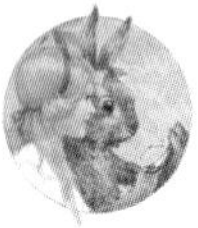

Alice did not quite know what to say to this: so she helped herself to some tea and bread-and-butter, and then turned to the Dormouse, and repeated her question. "Why did they live at the bottom of a well?"

The Dormouse again took a minute or two to think about it, and then said, "It was a treacle-well."

"There's no such thing!" Alice was beginning very angrily, but the Hatter and the March Hare went "Sh! sh!" and the Dormouse sulkily remarked, "If you can't be civil, you'd better finish the story for yourself."

"No, please go on!" Alice said. "I won't interrupt again. I dare say there may be *one*."

"One, indeed!" said the Dormouse indignantly. However, he consented to go on. "And so these three little sisters—they were learning to draw, you know—"

"What did they draw?" said Alice, quite forgetting her promise.

"Treacle," said the Dormouse, without considering at all this time.

"I want a clean cup," interrupted the Hatter: "let's all move one place on."

He moved on as he spoke, and the Dormouse followed him: the March Hare moved into the Dormouse's place, and Alice rather unwillingly took the place of the March Hare. The Hatter was the only one who got any advantage from the change: and Alice was a good deal worse off, as the March Hare had just upset the milk jug into his plate.

Alice did not wish to offend the Dormouse again, so she began very cautiously: "But I don't understand. Where did they draw the treacle from?"

"You can draw water out of a water-well," said the Hatter; "so I should think you could draw treacle out of a treacle-well— eh, stupid?"

"But they were *in* the well," Alice said to the Dormouse, not choosing to notice this last remark.

"Of course they were," said the Dormouse; "—well in."

This answer so confused poor Alice, that she let the Dormouse go on for some time without interrupting it.

"They were learning to draw," the Dormouse went on, yawning and rubbing its eyes, for it was getting very sleepy; "and they drew all manner of things—everything that begins with an M—"

"Why with an M?" said Alice.

"Why not?" said the March Hare.

Alice was silent.

The Dormouse had closed its eyes by this time, and was going off into a doze; but, on being pinched by the Hatter, it woke up again with a little shriek, and went on: "—that begins with an M, such as mouse-traps, and the moon, and memory, and muchness—you know you say things are 'much of a muchness'—did you ever see such a thing as a drawing of a muchness?"

"Really, now you ask me," said Alice, very much confused, "I don't think—"

"Then you shouldn't talk," said the Hatter.

This piece of rudeness was more than Alice could bear: she got up in great disgust, and walked off; the Dormouse fell asleep instantly, and neither of the others took the least notice of her going, though she looked back once or twice, half hoping that they would call after her: the last time she saw them, they were trying to put the Dormouse into the teapot.

upon Alice, as she stood watching them, and he checked himself suddenly: the others looked round also, and all of them bowed low.

"Would you tell me," said Alice, a little timidly, "why you are painting those roses?"

Five and Seven said nothing, but looked at Two. Two began in a low voice, "Why, the fact is, you see, miss, this here ought to have been a *red* rose tree, and we put a white one in by mistake; and if the Queen was to find it out, we should all have our heads cut off, you know. So you see, miss, we're doing our best, afore she comes, to—" At this moment, Five, who had been anxiously looking across the garden, called out, "The Queen! The Queen!" and the three gardeners instantly threw themselves flat upon their faces. There was a sound of many footsteps, and Alice looked round, eager to see the Queen.

First came ten soldiers carrying clubs: these were all shaped like the three gardeners, oblong and flat, with their hands and feet at the corners; next the ten courtiers: these were ornamented all over with diamonds, and walked two and two, as the soldiers did. After these came the royal children: there were ten of them, and the little dears came jumping merrily along hand in hand, in couples: they were all ornamented with hearts. Next came the guests, mostly Kings and Queens, and among them Alice recognised the White Rabbit: it was talking in a hurried, nervous manner, smiling at everything that was said, and went by without noticing her. Then followed the Knave of Hearts, carrying the King's crown on a crimson velvet cushion; and, last of all this grand procession, came THE KING AND QUEEN OF HEARTS.

Alice was rather doubtful whether she ought not to lie down on her face like the three gardeners, but she could not remember ever having heard of such a rule at processions; "and besides, what would be the use of a procession," thought she, "if people had all to lie down upon their faces, so that they couldn't see it?" So she stood still where she was, and waited.

When the procession came opposite to Alice, they all stopped and looked at her, and the Queen said severely, "Who is this?" She said it to the Knave of Hearts, who only bowed and smiled in reply.

"Idiot!" said the Queen, tossing her head impatiently; and, turning to Alice, she went on, "What's your name, child?"

"My name is Alice, so please your Majesty," said Alice very politely; but she added, to herself, "Why, they're only a pack of cards, after all. I needn't be afraid of them!"

"And who are *these*?" said the Queen, pointing to the three gardeners who were lying round the rose tree; for, you see, as they were lying on their faces, and the pattern on their backs was the same as the rest of the pack, she could not tell whether they were gardeners, or soldiers, or courtiers, or three of her own children.

"How should *I* know?" said Alice, surprised at her own courage. "It's no business of *mine*."

The Queen turned crimson with fury, and, after glaring at her for a moment like a wild beast, screamed, "Off with

her head! Off—"

"Nonsense!" said Alice, very loudly and decidedly, and the Queen was silent.

The King laid his hand upon her arm, and timidly said, "Consider, my dear: she is only a child!"

The Queen turned angrily away from him, and said to the Knave, "Turn them over!"

The Knave did so, very carefully, with one foot.

"Get up!" said the Queen, in a shrill, loud voice, and the three gardeners instantly jumped up, and began bowing to the King, the Queen, the royal children, and everybody else.

"Leave off that!" screamed the Queen. "You make me giddy." And then, turning to the rose tree, she went on, "What *have* you been doing here?"

"May it please your Majesty," said Two, in a very humble tone, going down on one knee as he spoke, "we were trying—"

"*I* see!" said the Queen, who had meanwhile been examining the roses. "Off with their heads!" and the procession moved on, three of the soldiers remaining behind to execute the unfortunate gardeners, who ran to Alice for protection.

"You shan't be beheaded!" said Alice, and she put them into a large flowerpot that stood near. The three soldiers

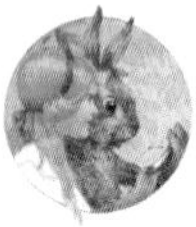

wandered about for a minute or two, looking for them, and then quietly marched off after the others.

"Are their heads off?" shouted the Queen.

"Their heads are gone, if it please your Majesty!" the soldiers shouted in reply.

"That's right!" shouted the Queen. "Can you play croquet?"

The soldiers were silent, and looked at Alice, as the question was evidently meant for her.

"Yes!" shouted Alice.

"Come on, then!" roared the Queen, and Alice joined the procession, wondering very much what would happen next.

"It's—it's a very fine day!" said a timid voice at her side. She was walking by the White Rabbit, who was peeping anxiously into her face.

"Very," said Alice: "—where's the Duchess?"

"Hush! Hush!" said the Rabbit in a low hurried tone. He looked anxiously over his shoulder as he spoke, and then raised himself upon tiptoe, put his mouth close to her ear, and whispered, "She's under sentence of execution."

"What for?" said Alice.

"Did you say, 'What a pity!?'" the Rabbit asked.

"No, I didn't," said Alice: "I don't think it's at all a pity. I said 'What for?'"

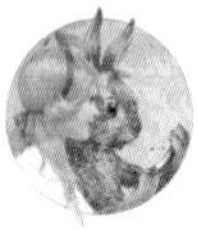

"She boxed the Queen's ears—" the Rabbit began. Alice gave a little scream of laughter. "Oh, hush!" the Rabbit whispered in a frightened tone. "The Queen will hear you! You see she came rather late, and the Queen said—"

"Get to your places!" shouted the Queen in a voice of thunder, and people began running about in all directions, tumbling up against each other; however, they got settled down in a minute or two, and the game began. Alice thought she had never seen such a curious croquet ground in her life: it was all ridges and furrows; the balls were live hedgehogs, the mallets live flamingoes, and the soldiers had to double themselves up and to stand upon their hands and feet, to make the arches.

The chief difficulty Alice found at first was in managing her flamingo: she succeeded in getting its body tucked away, comfortably enough, under her arm, with its legs hanging down, but generally, just as she had got its neck nicely straightened out, and was going to give the hedgehog a blow with its head, it *would* twist itself round and look up in her face, with such a puzzled expression that she could not help bursting out laughing; and when she had got its head down, and was going to begin again, it was very provoking to find that the hedgehog had unrolled itself, and was in the act of crawling away; besides all this, there was generally a ridge or furrow in the way wherever

she wanted to send the hedgehog to, and, as the doubled-up soldiers were always getting up and walking off to other parts of the ground, Alice soon came to the conclusion that it was a very difficult game indeed.

The players all played at once without waiting for turns, quarrelling all the while, and fighting for the hedgehogs; and in a very short time the Queen was in a furious passion, and went stamping about, and shouting "Off with his head!" or "Off with her head!" about once in a minute.

Alice began to feel very uneasy: to be sure she had not as yet had any dispute with the Queen, but she knew that it might happen any minute, "and then," thought she, "what would become of me? They're dreadfully fond of beheading people here; the great wonder is, that there's anyone left alive!"

She was looking about for some way of escape, and wondering whether she could get away without being seen, when she noticed a curious appearance in the air:

it puzzled her very much at first, but, after watching it a minute or two, she made it out to be a grin, and she said to herself, "It's the Cheshire Cat: now I shall have somebody to talk to."

"How are you getting on?" said the Cat, as soon as there was mouth enough for it to speak with.

Alice waited till the eyes appeared, and then nodded. "It's no use speaking to it," she thought, "till its ears have come, or at least one of them." In another minute the whole head appeared, and then Alice put down her flamingo, and began an account of the game, feeling very glad she had someone to listen to her. The Cat seemed to think that there was enough of it now in sight, and no more of it appeared.

"I don't think they play at all fairly," Alice began, in rather a complaining tone, "and they all quarrel so dreadfully one can't hear oneself speak—and they don't seem to have any rules in particular; at least, if there are, nobody attends to them—and you've no idea how confusing it is all the things being alive; for instance, there's the arch I've got to go through next walking about at the other end of the ground—and I should have croqueted the Queen's hedgehog just now, only it ran away when it saw mine coming!"

"How do you like the Queen?" said the Cat in a low voice.

"Not at all," said Alice: "she's so extremely—" Just then she noticed that the Queen was close behind her listening: so she went on, "—likely to win, that it's hardly worth while finishing the game."

The Queen smiled and passed on.

"Who *are* you talking to?" said the King, coming up to Alice, and looking at the Cat's head with great curiosity.

"It's a friend of mine—a Cheshire Cat," said Alice: "allow me to introduce it."

"I don't like the look of it at all," said the King: "however, it may kiss my hand if it likes."

"I'd rather not," the Cat remarked.

"Don't be impertinent," said the King, "and don't look at me like that!" He got behind Alice as he spoke.

"A cat may look at a king," said Alice. "I've read that in some book, but I don't remember where."

"Well, it must be removed," said the King very decidedly, and he called to the Queen, who was passing at the moment, "My dear! I wish you would have this cat removed!"

The Queen had only one way of settling all difficulties, great or small. "Off with his head!" she said, without even looking round.

"I'll fetch the executioner myself," said the King eagerly, and he hurried off.

Alice thought she might as well go back and see how

the game was going on, as she heard the Queen's voice in the distance, screaming with passion. She had already heard her sentence three of the players to be executed for having missed their turns, and she did not like the look of things at all, as the game was in such confusion that she never knew whether it was her turn or not. So she went in search of her hedgehog.

The hedgehog was engaged in a fight with another hedgehog, which seemed to Alice an excellent opportunity for croqueting one of them with the other: the only difficulty was that her flamingo was gone across to the other side of the garden, where Alice could see it trying in a helpless sort of way to fly up into one of the trees.

By the time she had caught the flamingo and brought it back, the fight was over, and both the hedgehogs were out of sight: "but it doesn't matter much," thought Alice, "as all the arches are gone from this side of the ground." So she tucked it under her arm, that it might not escape again, and went back for a little more conversation with her friend.

When she got back to the Cheshire Cat, she was surprised to find quite a large crowd collected round it: there was a dispute going on between the executioner, the King and the Queen, who were all talking at once, while all the rest were quite silent, and looked very uncomfortable.

The moment Alice appeared, she was appealed to by all three to settle the question, and they repeated their arguments to her, though, as they all spoke at once, she found it very hard indeed to make out exactly what they said.

The executioner's argument was that you couldn't cut off a head unless there was a body to cut it off from: that he had never had to do such a thing before, and he wasn't going to begin at *his* time of life.

The King's argument was that anything that had a head could be beheaded, and that you weren't to talk nonsense.

The Queen's argument was that if something wasn't done about it in less than no time, she'd have everybody executed, all round. (It was this last remark that had made the whole party look so grave and anxious.)

Alice could think of nothing else to say but, "It belongs to the Duchess: you'd better ask *her* about it."

"She's in prison," the Queen said to the executioner: "fetch her here." And the executioner went off like an arrow.

The Cat's head began fading away the moment he was gone, and, by the time he had come back with the Duchess, it had entirely disappeared; so the King and the executioner ran wildly up and down looking for it, while the rest of the party went back to the game.

Chapter 9

The Mock Turtle's Story

You can't think how glad I am to see you again, you dear old thing!" said the Duchess, as she tucked her arm affectionately into Alice's, and they walked off together.

Alice was very glad to find her in such a pleasant temper, and thought to herself that perhaps it was only the pepper that had made her so savage when they met in the kitchen.

"When *I'm* a Duchess," she said to herself (not in a very hopeful tone though), "I won't have any pepper in my kitchen *at all*. Soup does very well without—Maybe it's always pepper that makes people hot-tempered," she went on, very much pleased at having found out a new kind of rule, "and vinegar that makes them sour—and camomile that makes them bitter—and—and barley-sugar and such things that make children sweet-tempered. I only wish people knew *that*: then they wouldn't be so stingy about it, you know—"

She had quite forgotten the Duchess by this time, and was a little startled when she heard her voice close to her ear. "You're thinking about something, my dear, and that

makes you forget to talk. I can't tell you just now what the moral of that is, but I shall remember it in a bit."

"Perhaps it hasn't one," Alice ventured to remark.

"Tut, tut, child!" said the Duchess. "Everything's got a moral, if only you can find it." And she squeezed herself up closer to Alice's side as she spoke.

Alice did not much like keeping so close to her: first, because the Duchess was *very* ugly; and secondly, because she was exactly the right height to rest her chin upon Alice's shoulder, and it was an uncomfortably sharp chin. However, she did not like to be rude, so she bore it as well as she could. "The game seems to be going on rather better now," she said.

" 'Tis so," said the Duchess: "and the moral of it is—'Oh, 'tis love, 'tis love, that makes the world go round!'"

"Somebody said," whispered Alice, "that it's done by everybody minding their own business!"

"Ah, well! It means much the same thing," said the Duchess, digging her sharp little chin into Alice's shoulder as she added, "and the moral of *that* is—'Take care of the sense, and the sounds will take care of themselves.'"

"How fond she is of finding morals in things!" Alice thought to herself.

"I dare say you're wondering why I don't put my arm round your waist," the Duchess said after a pause: "the reason is that I'm doubtful about the temper of your flamingo. Shall I try the experiment?"

"He might bite!" Alice cautiously replied, not feeling at all anxious to have the experiment tried.

"Very true," said the Duchess: "flamingoes and mustard both bite. And the moral of that is—'Birds of a feather flock together.'"

"Only mustard isn't a bird," Alice remarked.

"Right, as usual," said the Duchess: "what a clear way you have of putting things!"

"It's a mineral, I *think*," said Alice.

"Of course it is," said the Duchess, who seemed ready to agree to everything that Alice said; "there's a large mustard-mine near here. And the moral of that is—'The more there is of mine, the less there is of yours.'"

"Oh, I know!" exclaimed Alice, who had not attended to this last remark. "It's a vegetable. It doesn't look like one, but it is."

"I quite agree with you," said the Duchess; "and the moral of that is—'Be what you would seem to be'—or if you'd like it put more simply—'Never imagine yourself not to be otherwise than what it might appear to others that what you were or might have been was not otherwise than what you had been would have appeared to them to be otherwise.'"

"I think I should understand that better," Alice said very politely, "if I had it written down: but I'm afraid I can't quite follow it as you say it."

"That's nothing to what I could say if I chose," the Duchess replied, in a pleased tone.

"Pray don't trouble yourself to say it any longer than that," said Alice.

"Oh, don't talk about trouble!" said the Duchess. "I make you a present of everything I've said as yet."

"A cheap sort of present!" thought Alice. "I'm glad they don't give birthday presents like that!" But she did not venture to say it out loud.

"Thinking again?" the Duchess asked with another dig of her sharp little chin.

"I've a right to think," said Alice sharply, for she was beginning to feel a little worried.

"Just about as much right," said the Duchess, "as pigs have to fly; and the m—"

But here, to Alice's great surprise, the Duchess's voice died away, even in the middle of her favourite word "moral," and the arm that was linked into hers began to tremble. Alice looked up, and there stood the Queen in front of them, with her arms folded, frowning like a thunderstorm.

"A fine day, your Majesty!" the Duchess began in a low, weak voice.

"Now, I give you fair warning," shouted the Queen, stamping on the ground as she spoke; "either you or your head must be off, and that in about half no time! Take your choice!"

The Duchess took her choice, and was gone in a moment.

"Let's go on with the game," the Queen said to Alice; and Alice was too much frightened to say a word, but slowly followed her back to the croquet ground.

The other guests had taken advantage of the Queen's absence, and were resting in the shade; however, the moment they saw her, they hurried back to the game, the Queen merely remarking that a moment's delay would cost them their lives.

All the time they were playing the Queen never left off quarrelling with the other players, and shouting "Off with his head!" or "Off with her head!" Those whom she sentenced were taken into custody by the soldiers, who of course had to leave off being arches to do this, so that by the end of half an hour or so there were no arches left, and all the players, except the King, the Queen and Alice, were in custody and under sentence of execution.

Then the Queen left off, quite out of breath, and said to Alice, "Have you seen the Mock Turtle yet?"

"No," said Alice. "I don't even know what a Mock Turtle is."

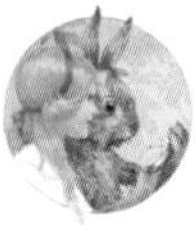

"It's the thing Mock Turtle Soup is made from," said the Queen.

"I never saw one, or heard of one," said Alice.

"Come on, then," said the Queen, "and he shall tell you his history."

As they walked off together, Alice heard the King say in a low voice, to the company generally, "You are all pardoned." "Come, *that's* a good thing!" she said to herself, for she had felt quite unhappy at the number of executions the Queen had ordered.

They very soon came upon a Gryphon, lying fast asleep in the sun. (If you don't know what a Gryphon is, look at the picture.) "Up, lazy thing!" said the Queen, "and take this young lady to see the Mock Turtle, and to hear his history. I must go back and see after some executions I have ordered," and she walked off, leaving Alice alone with the Gryphon. Alice did not quite like the look of the creature, but on the whole she thought it would be quite as safe to stay with it as to go after that savage Queen: so she waited.

The Gryphon sat up and rubbed its eyes: then it watched the Queen till she was out of sight: then it chuckled. "What fun!" said the Gryphon, half to itself, half to Alice.

"What *is* the fun?" said Alice.

"Why, *she*," said the Gryphon. "It's all her fancy, that:

they never executes nobody, you know. Come on!"

"Everybody says 'come on!' here," thought Alice, as she went slowly after it: "I never was so ordered about in all my life, never!"

They had not gone far before they saw the Mock Turtle in the distance, sitting sad and lonely on a little ledge of rock, and, as they came nearer, Alice could hear him sighing as if his heart would break. She pitied him deeply. "What is his sorrow?" she asked the Gryphon, and the Gryphon answered, very nearly in the same words as before, "It's all his fancy, that: he hasn't got no sorrow, you know. Come on!"

So they went up to the Mock Turtle, who looked at them with large eyes full of tears, but said nothing.

"This here young lady," said the Gryphon, "she wants for to know your history, she do."

"I'll tell it her," said the Mock Turtle in a deep, hollow tone: "sit down, both of you, and don't speak a word till I've finished."

So they sat down, and nobody spoke for some minutes. Alice thought to herself, "I don't see how he can *ever* finish, if he doesn't begin." But she waited patiently.

"Once," said the Mock Turtle at last, with a deep sigh, "I was a real Turtle."

These words were followed by a very long silence,

broken only by an occasional exclamation of "Hjckrrh!" from the Gryphon, and the constant heavy sobbing of the Mock Turtle. Alice was very nearly getting up and saying, "Thank you, sir, for your interesting story," but she could not help thinking there *must* be more to come, so she sat still and said nothing.

"When we were little," the Mock Turtle went on at last, more calmly, though still sobbing a little now and then, "we went to school in the sea. The master was an old Turtle—we used to call him Tortoise—"

"Why did you call him Tortoise, if he wasn't one?" Alice asked.

"We called him Tortoise because he taught us," said the Mock Turtle angrily: "really you are very dull!"

"You ought to be ashamed of yourself for asking such a simple question," added the Gryphon; and then they both sat silent and looked at poor Alice, who felt ready to sink into the earth. At last the Gryphon said to the Mock Turtle, "Drive on, old fellow! Don't be all day about it!" and he went on in these words:

"Yes, we went to school in the sea, though you mayn't believe it—"

"I never said I didn't!" interrupted Alice.

"You did," said the Mock Turtle.

"Hold your tongue!" added the Gryphon, before Alice could speak again. The Mock Turtle went on —

"We had the best of educations—in fact, we went to school every day—"

"*I've* been to a day-school, too," said Alice; "you needn't be so proud as all that."

"With extras?" asked the Mock Turtle a little anxiously.

"Yes," said Alice, "we learned French and music."

"And washing?" said the Mock Turtle.

"Certainly not!" said Alice indignantly.

"Ah! then yours wasn't a really good school," said the Mock Turtle in a tone of great relief. "Now at *ours* they had at the end of the bill, 'French, music, *and washing*—extra.'"

"You couldn't have wanted it much," said Alice; "living at the bottom of the sea."

"I couldn't afford to learn it," said the Mock Turtle with a sigh. "I only took the regular course."

"What was that?" enquired Alice.

"Reeling and Writhing, of course, to begin with," the Mock Turtle replied; "and then the different branches of Arithmetic—Ambition, Distraction, Uglification and Derision."

"I never heard of 'Uglification,'" Alice ventured to say. "What is it?"

The Gryphon lifted up both its paws in surprise. "What! Never heard of uglifying!" it exclaimed. "You know what to beautify is, I suppose?"

"Yes," said Alice doubtfully: "it means—to—make—anything—prettier."

"Well, then," the Gryphon went on, "if you don't know what to uglify is, you must be a simpleton."

Alice did not feel encouraged to ask any more questions about it, so she turned to the Mock Turtle, and said, "What else had you to learn?"

"Well, there was Mystery," the Mock Turtle replied, counting off the subjects on his flappers, "—Mystery, ancient and modern, with Seaography; then Drawling—the Drawling-master was an old conger-eel, that used to come once a week: *he* taught us Drawling, Stretching and Fainting in Coils."

"What was *that* like?" said Alice.

"Well, I can't show it you myself," the Mock Turtle said: "I'm too stiff. And the Gryphon never learnt it."

"Hadn't time," said the Gryphon: "I went to the Classical master, though. He was an old crab, *he* was."

"I never went to him," the Mock Turtle said with a sigh: "he taught Laughing and Grief, they used to say."

"So he did, so he did," said the Gryphon, sighing in his turn; and both creatures hid their faces in their paws.

"And how many hours a day did you do lessons?" said Alice, in a hurry to change the subject.

"Ten hours the first day," said the Mock Turtle; "nine the next, and so on."

"What a curious plan!" exclaimed Alice.

"That's the reason they're called lessons," the Gryphon remarked: "because they lessen from day to day."

This was quite a new idea to Alice, and she thought it over a little before she made her next remark. "Then the eleventh day must have been a holiday?"

"Of course it was," said the Mock Turtle.

"And how did you manage on the twelfth?" Alice went on eagerly.

"That's enough about lessons," the Gryphon interrupted in a very decided tone: "tell her something about the games now."

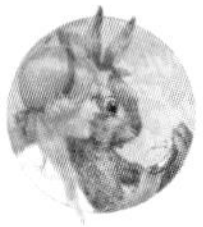

Chapter 10

The Lobster Quadrille

The Mock Turtle sighed deeply, and drew the back of one flapper across his eyes. He looked at Alice, and tried to speak, but, for a minute or two, sobs choked his voice. "Same as if he had a bone in his throat," said the Gryphon: and it set to work shaking him and punching him in the back. At last the Mock Turtle recovered his voice, and, with tears running down his cheeks, went on again—

"You may not have lived much under the sea—" ("I haven't," said Alice) "and perhaps you were never even introduced to a lobster—" (Alice began to say, "I once tasted—" but checked herself hastily, and said, "No, never") "—so you can have no idea what a delightful thing a Lobster Quadrille is!"

"No, indeed," said Alice. "What sort of a dance is it?"

"Why," said the Gryphon, "you first form into a line along the seashore—"

"Two lines!" cried the Mock Turtle. "Seals, turtles, and so on; then, when you've cleared the jellyfish out of the way—"

"*That* generally takes some time," interrupted the Gryphon. "—you advance twice—"

"Each with a lobster as a partner!" cried the Gryphon.

"Of course," the Mock Turtle said: "advance twice, set to partners—"

"—change lobsters, and retire in same order," continued the Gryphon.

"Then, you know," the Mock Turtle went on, "you throw the—"

"The lobsters!" shouted the Gryphon, with a bound into the air.

"—as far out to sea as you can—"

"Swim after them!" screamed the Gryphon.

"Turn a somersault in the sea!" cried the Mock Turtle, capering wildly about.

"Change lobsters again!" yelled the Gryphon.

"Back to land again, and—that's all the first figure," said the Mock Turtle, suddenly dropping his voice; and the two creatures, who had been jumping about like mad things, sat down again very sadly and quietly, and looked at Alice.

"It must be a very pretty dance," said Alice, timidly.

"Would you like to see a little of it?" said the Mock Turtle.

"Very much indeed," said Alice.

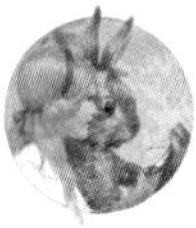

"Let's try the first figure!" said the Mock Turtle to the Gryphon. "We can do without lobsters, you know. Which shall sing?"

"Oh, *you* sing," said the Gryphon. "I've forgotten the words."

So they began solemnly dancing round and round Alice, every now and then treading on her toes when they passed too close, and waving their forepaws to mark the time, while the Mock Turtle sang this, very slowly and sadly—

"'Will you walk a little faster?' said a whiting to a snail.
'There's a porpoise close behind us, and he's treading on my tail.
See how eagerly the lobsters and the turtles all advance!
They are waiting on the shingle—will you come and join the dance?
Will you, won't you, will you, won't you, will you join the dance?
Will you, won't you, will you, won't you, won't you join the dance?

'You can really have no notion how delightful it will be,
When they take us up and throw us, with the lobsters, out to sea!'
But the snail replied, 'Too far, too far!' and gave a look askance—
Said he thanked the whiting kindly, but he would not join the dance.
Would not, could not, would not, could not, would not join the dance.
Would not, could not, would not, could not, could not join the dance.

'What matters it how far we go?' his scaly friend replied.
'There is another shore, you know, upon the other side.
The further off from England the nearer is to France—
Then turn not pale, beloved snail, but come and join the dance.
Will you, won't you, will you, won't you, will you join the dance?
Will you, won't you, will you, won't you, won't you join the dance?'"

"Thank you, it's a very interesting dance to watch," said Alice, feeling very glad that it was over at last: "and I do so like that curious song about the whiting!"

"Oh, as to the whiting," said the Mock Turtle, "they—you've seen them, of course?"

"Yes," said Alice, "I've often seen them at dinn—" she checked herself hastily.

"I don't know where Dinn may be," said the Mock Turtle, "but if you've seen them so often, of course you know what they're like."

"I believe so," Alice replied thoughtfully. "They have their tails in their mouths—and they're all over crumbs."

"You're wrong about the crumbs," said the Mock Turtle: "crumbs would all wash off in the sea. But they *have* their tails in their mouths; and the reason is—" here the Mock Turtle yawned and shut his eyes. "Tell her about the reason and all that," he said to the Gryphon.

"The reason is," said the Gryphon, "that they *would* go with the lobsters to the dance. So they got thrown out to sea. So they had to fall a long way. So they got their tails fast in their mouths. So they couldn't get them out again. That's all."

"Thank you," said Alice, "it's very interesting. I never knew so much about a whiting before."

"I can tell you more than that, if you like," said the Gryphon. "Do you know why it's called a whiting?"

"I never thought about it," said Alice. "Why?"

"*It does the boots and shoes,*" the Gryphon replied very solemnly.

Alice was thoroughly puzzled. "Does the boots and shoes!" she repeated in a wondering tone.

"Why, what are *your* shoes done with?" said the Gryphon. "I mean, what makes them so shiny?"

Alice looked down at them, and considered a little before she gave her answer. "They're done with blacking, I believe."

"Boots and shoes under the sea," the Gryphon went on in a deep voice, "are done with a whiting. Now you know."

"And what are they made of?" Alice asked in a tone of great curiosity.

"Soles and eels, of course," the Gryphon replied rather impatiently: "any shrimp could have told you that."

"If I'd been the whiting," said Alice, whose thoughts were still running on the song, "I'd have said to the

porpoise, 'Keep back, please: we don't want *you* with us!'"

"They were obliged to have him with them," the Mock Turtle said: "no wise fish would go anywhere without a porpoise."

"Wouldn't it really?" said Alice in a tone of great surprise.

"Of course not," said the Mock Turtle: "why, if a fish came to *me*, and told me he was going a journey, I should say 'With what porpoise?'"

"Don't you mean 'purpose'?" said Alice.

"I mean what I say," the Mock Turtle replied in an offended tone. And the Gryphon added, "Come, let's hear some of *your* adventures."

"I could tell you my adventures—beginning from this morning," said Alice a little timidly: "but it's no use going back to yesterday, because I was a different person then."

"Explain all that," said the Mock Turtle.

"No, no! The adventures first," said the Gryphon in an impatient tone: "explanations take such a dreadful time."

So Alice began telling them her adventures from the time when she first saw the White Rabbit. She was a little nervous about it just at first, the two creatures got so close to her, one on each side, and opened their eyes and mouths so *very* wide, but she gained courage as she went on. Her listeners were perfectly quiet till she got to the part about her repeating "*You are old, Father William*" to the Caterpillar, and the words all coming different, and then the Mock Turtle drew a long breath, and said, "That's very curious."

"It's all about as curious as it can be," said the Gryphon.

"It all came different!" the Mock Turtle repeated thoughtfully. "I should like to hear her repeat something now. Tell her to begin." He looked at the Gryphon as if he thought it had some kind of authority over Alice.

"Stand up and repeat ' '*Tis the voice of the sluggard*,'" said the Gryphon.

"How the creatures order one about, and make one repeat lessons!" thought Alice. "I might as well be at school at once." However, she got up, and began to repeat it, but her head was so full of the Lobster Quadrille, that she hardly knew what she was saying, and the words came very queer indeed —

" 'Tis the voice of the Lobster; I heard him declare,
'You have baked me too brown, I must sugar my hair.'
As a duck with its eyelids, so he with his nose
Trims his belt and his buttons, and turns out his toes.
When the sands are all dry, he is gay as a lark,
And will talk in contemptuous tone of the Shark:
But, when the tide rises and sharks are around,
His voice has a timid and tremulous sound."

"That's different from what *I* used to say when I was a child," said the Gryphon.

"Well, I never heard it before," said the Mock Turtle; "but it sounds uncommon nonsense."

Alice said nothing; she had sat down with her face in her hands, wondering if anything would *ever* happen in a natural way again.

"I should like to have it explained," said the Mock Turtle.

"She can't explain it," said the Gryphon hastily. "Go on to the next verse."

"But about his toes?" the Mock Turtle persisted. "How *could* he turn them out with his nose, you know?"

"It's the first position in dancing." Alice said; but was dreadfully puzzled by it all, and longed to change the subject.

"Go on with the next verse," the Gryphon repeated: "it begins with the words '*I passed by his garden.*'"

Alice did not dare to disobey, though she felt sure it would all come wrong, and she went on in a trembling voice —

"I passed by his garden, and marked, with one eye,
How the Owl and the Panther were sharing a pie:
The Panther took pie-crust, and gravy, and meat,
While the Owl had the dish as its share of the treat.
When the pie was all finished, the Owl, as a boon,
Was kindly permitted to pocket the spoon:

While the Panther received knife and fork with a growl,
And concluded the banquet —"

"What *is* the use of repeating all that stuff," the Mock Turtle interrupted, "if you don't explain it as you go on? It's by far the most confusing thing *I* ever heard!"

"Yes, I think you'd better leave off," said the Gryphon: and Alice was only too glad to do so.

"Shall we try another figure of the Lobster Quadrille?" the Gryphon went on. "Or would you like the Mock Turtle to sing you a song?"

"Oh, a song, please, if the Mock Turtle would be so kind," Alice replied, so eagerly that the Gryphon said, in a rather offended tone. "Hm! No accounting for tastes! Sing her *Turtle Soup*, will you, old fellow?"

The Mock Turtle sighed deeply, and began, in a voice sometimes choked with sobs, to sing this—

"Beautiful Soup, so rich and green,
Waiting in a hot tureen!
Who for such dainties would not stoop?
Soup of the evening, beautiful Soup!
Soup of the evening, beautiful Soup!
Beau —ootiful Soo — oop!
Beau —ootiful Soo — oop!

Soo – oop of the e– e – evening,
Beautiful, beautiful Soup!

Beautiful Soup! Who cares for fish,
Game, or any other dish?
Who would not give all else for two
Pennyworth only of beautiful Soup?
Pennyworth only of beautiful Soup?
Beau —ootiful Soo —oop!
Beau —ootiful Soo —oop!
Soo —oop of the e —e —evening,
Beautiful, beauty —FUL SOUP!"

"Chorus again!" cried the Gryphon, and the Mock Turtle had just begun to repeat it, when a cry of "The trial's beginning!" was heard in the distance.

"Come on!" cried the Gryphon, and, taking Alice by the hand, it hurried off, without waiting for the end of the song.

"What trial is it?" Alice panted as she ran; but the Gryphon only answered, "Come on!" and ran the faster, while more and more faintly came, carried on the breeze that followed them, the melancholy words–

"Soo—oop of the e—e—evening,
Beautiful, beautiful Soup!

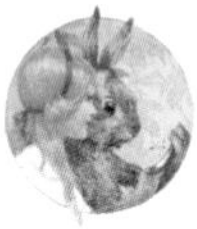

Chapter 11

Who Stole the Tarts?

The King and Queen of Hearts were seated on their throne when they arrived, with a great crowd assembled about them—all sorts of little birds and beasts, as well as the whole pack of cards: the Knave was standing before them, in chains, with a soldier on each side to guard him; and near the King was the White Rabbit, with a trumpet in one hand, and a scroll of parchment in the other. In the very middle of the court was a table, with a large dish of tarts upon it: they looked so good, that it made Alice quite hungry to look at them—"I wish they'd get the trial done," she thought, "and hand round the refreshments!" But there seemed to be no chance of this, so she began looking about her, to pass away the time.

Alice had never been in a court of justice before, but she had read about them in books, and she was quite pleased to find that she knew the name of nearly everything there. "That's the judge," she said to herself, "because of his great wig."

The judge, by the way, was the King; and as he wore his

crown over the wig (look at the frontispiece if you want to see how he did it), he did not look at all comfortable, and it was certainly not becoming.

"And that's the jury-box," thought Alice, "and those twelve creatures," (she was obliged to say "creatures," you see, because some of them were animals, and some were birds), "I suppose they are the jurors." She said this last word two or three times over to herself, being rather proud of it: for she thought, and rightly too, that very few little girls of her age knew the meaning of it at all. However, "jurymen" would have done just as well.

The twelve jurors were all writing very busily on slates. "What are they all doing?" Alice whispered to the Gryphon. "They can't have anything to put down yet, before the trial's begun."

"They're putting down their names," the Gryphon whispered in reply, "for fear they should forget them before the end of the trial."

"Stupid things!" Alice began in a loud, indignant voice, but she stopped hastily, for the White Rabbit cried out, "Silence in the court!" and the King put on his spectacles and looked anxiously round, to see who was talking.

Alice could see, as well as if she were looking over their shoulders, that all the jurors were writing down "stupid things!" on their slates, and she could even make out that

one of them didn't know how to spell "stupid," and that he had to ask his neighbour to tell him. "A nice muddle their slates will be in before the trial's over!" thought Alice.

One of the jurors had a pencil that squeaked. This, of course, Alice could *not* stand, and she went round the court and got behind him, and very soon found an opportunity of taking it away. She did it so quickly that the poor little juror (it was Bill, the Lizard) could not make out at all what had become of it so, after hunting all about for it, he was obliged to write with one finger for the rest of the day; and this was of very little use, as it left no mark on the slate.

"Herald, read the accusation!" said the King.

On this the White Rabbit blew three blasts on the trumpet, and then unrolled the parchment scroll, and read as follows—

"The Queen of Hearts, she made some tarts,
All on a summer day:
The Knave of Hearts, he stole those tarts,
And took them quite away!"

"Consider your verdict," the King said to the jury.

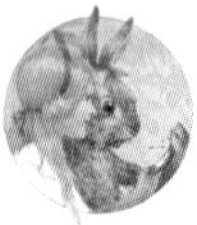

"Not yet, not yet!" the Rabbit hastily interrupted. "There's a great deal to come before that!"

"Call the first witness," said the King; and the White Rabbit blew three blasts on the trumpet, and called out, "First witness!"

The first witness was the Hatter. He came in with a teacup in one hand and a piece of bread-and-butter in the other. "I beg pardon, your Majesty," he began, "for bringing these in: but I hadn't quite finished my tea when I was sent for."

"You ought to have finished," said the King. "When did you begin?"

The Hatter looked at the March Hare, who had followed him into the court, arm in arm with the Dormouse. "Fourteenth of March, I *think* it was," he said.

"Fifteenth," said the March Hare.

"Sixteenth," added the Dormouse.

"Write that down," the King said to the jury, and the jury eagerly wrote down all three dates on their slates, and then added them up, and reduced the answer to shillings and pence.

"Take off your hat," the King said to the Hatter.

"It isn't mine," said the Hatter.

"*Stolen*!" the King exclaimed, turning to the jury, who instantly made a memorandum of the fact.

THIS STYLE
10/6
SILENCE
IN
THE

"I keep them to sell," the Hatter added as an explanation: "I've none of my own. I'm a hatter."

Here the Queen put on her spectacles, and began staring hard at the Hatter, who turned pale and fidgeted.

"Give your evidence," said the King; "and don't be nervous, or I'll have you executed on the spot."

This did not seem to encourage the witness at all; he kept shifting from one foot to the other, looking uneasily at the Queen, and in his confusion he bit a large piece out of his teacup instead of the bread-and-butter.

Just at this moment Alice felt a very curious sensation, which puzzled her a good deal until she made out what it was: she was beginning to grow larger again, and she thought at first she would get up and leave the court; but on second thoughts she decided to remain where she was as long as there was room for her.

"I wish you wouldn't squeeze so." said the Dormouse, who was sitting next to her. "I can hardly breathe."

"I can't help it," said Alice very meekly: "I'm growing."

"You've no right to grow *here*," said the Dormouse.

"Don't talk nonsense," said Alice more boldly: "you know you're growing too."

"Yes, but *I* grow at a reasonable pace," said the Dormouse: "not in that ridiculous fashion." And he got up very sulkily and crossed over to the other side of the court.

All this time the Queen had never left off staring at the Hatter, and, just as the Dormouse crossed the court, she said to one of the officers of the court, "Bring me the list of the singers in the last concert!" on which the wretched Hatter trembled so, that he shook both his shoes off.

"Give your evidence," the King repeated angrily, "or I'll have you executed, whether you're nervous or not."

"I'm a poor man, your Majesty," the Hatter began, in a trembling voice, "—and I hadn't begun my tea—not above a week or so—and what with the bread-and-butter getting so thin—and the twinkling of the tea—"

"The twinkling of the *what*?" said the King.

"It *began* with the tea," the Hatter replied.

"Of course twinkling begins with a T!" said the King sharply. "Do you take me for a dunce? Go on!"

"I'm a poor man," the Hatter went on, "and most things twinkled after that—only the March Hare said—"

"I didn't!" the March Hare interrupted in a great hurry.

"You did!" said the Hatter.

"I deny it!" said the March Hare.

"He denies it," said the King: "leave out that part."

"Well, at any rate, the Dormouse said—" the Hatter went on, looking anxiously round to see if he would deny it too: but the Dormouse denied nothing, being fast asleep.

"After that," continued the Hatter, "I cut some more bread-and-butter—"

"But what did the Dormouse say?" one of the jury asked.

"That I can't remember," said the Hatter.

"You *must* remember," remarked the King, "or I'll have you executed."

The miserable Hatter dropped his teacup and bread-and-butter, and went down on one knee. "I'm a poor man, your Majesty," he began.

"You're a *very* poor *speaker*," said the King.

Here one of the guinea-pigs cheered, and was immediately suppressed by the officers of the court. (As that is rather a hard word, I will just explain to you how it was done. They had a large canvas bag, which tied up at the mouth with strings: into this they slipped the guinea-pig, head first, and then sat upon it.)

"I'm glad I've seen that done," thought Alice. "I've so often read in the newspapers, at the end of trials, 'There

was some attempts at applause, which was immediately suppressed by the officers of the court,' and I never understood what it meant till now."

"If that's all you know about it, you may stand down," continued the King.

"I can't go no lower," said the Hatter: "I'm on the floor, as it is."

"Then you may *sit* down," the King replied.

Here the other guinea-pig cheered, and was suppressed.

"Come, that finishes the guinea-pigs!" thought Alice. "Now we shall get on better."

"I'd rather finish my tea," said the Hatter, with an anxious look at the Queen, who was reading the list of singers.

"You may go," said the King; and the Hatter hurriedly left the court, without even waiting to put his shoes on.

"—and just take his head off outside," the Queen added to one of the officers; but the Hatter was out of sight before the officer could get to the door.

"Call the next witness!" said the King.

The next witness was the Duchess's cook. She carried the pepper-box in her hand, and Alice guessed who it was, even before she got into the court, by the way the people near the door began sneezing all at once.

"Give your evidence," said the King.

"Shan't," said the cook.

The King looked anxiously at the White Rabbit, who said in a low voice, "Your Majesty must cross-examine *this* witness."

"Well, if I must, I must," the King said with a melancholy air, and, after folding his arms and frowning at the cook till his eyes were nearly out of sight, he said in a deep voice, "What are tarts made of?"

"Pepper, mostly," said the cook.

"Treacle," said a sleepy voice behind her.

"Collar that Dormouse," the Queen shrieked out. "Behead that Dormouse! Turn that Dormouse out of court! Suppress him! Pinch him! Off with his whiskers!"

For some minutes the whole court was in confusion, getting the Dormouse turned out, and, by the time they had settled down again, the cook had disappeared.

"Never mind!" said the King, with an air of great relief. "Call the next witness." And he added in an undertone to the Queen, "Really, my dear, *you* must cross-examine the next witness. It quite makes my forehead ache!"

Alice watched the White Rabbit as he fumbled over the list, feeling very curious to see what the next witness would be like, "—for they haven't got much evidence *yet*," she said to herself. Imagine her surprise, when the White Rabbit read out, at the top of his shrill little voice, the name "Alice!"

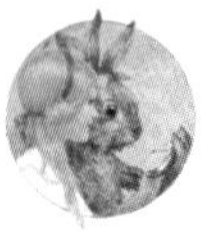

Chapter 12

Alice's Evidence

"Here!" cried Alice, quite forgetting in the flurry of the moment how large she had grown in the last few minutes, and she jumped up in such a hurry that she tipped over the jury-box with the edge of her skirt, upsetting all the jurymen on to the heads of the crowd below, and there they lay sprawling about, reminding her very much of a globe of goldfish she had accidentally upset the week before.

"Oh, I *beg* your pardon!" she exclaimed in a tone of great dismay, and began picking them up again as quickly as she could, for the accident of the goldfish kept running in her head, and she had a vague sort of idea that they must be collected at once and put back into the jury-box, or they would die.

"The trial cannot proceed," said the King in a very grave voice, "until all the jurymen are back in their proper places—*all*," he repeated with great emphasis, looking hard at Alice as he said so.

Alice looked at the jury-box, and saw that, in her haste, she had put the Lizard in head downwards, and the poor little thing was waving its tail about in a melancholy way,

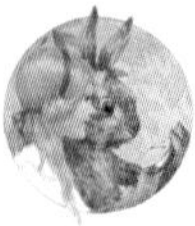

being quite unable to move. She soon got it out again, and put it right; "not that it signifies much," she said to herself; "I should think it would be *quite* as much use in the trial one way up as the other."

As soon as the jury had a little recovered from the shock of being upset, and their slates and pencils had been found and handed back to them, they set to work very diligently to write out a history of the accident, all except the Lizard, who seemed too much overcome to do anything but sit with its mouth open, gazing up into the roof of the court.

"What do you know about this business?" the King said to Alice.

"Nothing," said Alice.

"Nothing *whatever*?" persisted the King.

"Nothing whatever," said Alice.

"That's very important," the King said, turning to the jury. They were just beginning to write this down on their slates, when the White Rabbit interrupted: "*Un*important, your Majesty means, of course," he said in a very respectful tone, but frowning and making faces at him as he spoke.

"*Un*important, of course, I meant," the King said hastily, and went on to himself in an undertone, "important—unimportant—unimportant—important—" as if he were trying which word sounded best.

Some of the jury wrote it down "important," and some "unimportant." Alice could see this, as she was near enough to look over their slates; "but it doesn't matter a bit," she thought to herself.

At this moment the King, who had been for some time busily writing in his notebook, cackled out "Silence!" and read out from his book, "Rule Forty-two. *All persons more than a mile high to leave the court*."

Everybody looked at Alice.

"*I'm* not a mile high," said Alice.

"You are," said the King.

"Nearly two miles high," added the Queen.

"Well, I shan't go, at any rate," said Alice: "besides, that's not a regular rule: you invented it just now."

"It's the oldest rule in the book," said the King.

"Then it ought to be Number One," said Alice.

The King turned pale, and shut his notebook hastily. "Consider your verdict," he said to the jury, in a low trembling voice.

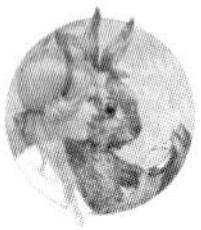

"There's more evidence to come yet, please your Majesty," said the White Rabbit, jumping up in a great hurry: "this paper has just been picked up."

"What's in it?" said the Queen.

"I haven't opened it yet," said the White Rabbit, "but it seems to be a letter, written by the prisoner to—to somebody."

"It must have been that," said the King, "unless it was written to nobody, which isn't usual, you know."

"Who is it directed to?" said one of the jurymen.

"It isn't directed at all," said the White Rabbit; "in fact, there's nothing written on the *outside*." He unfolded the paper as he spoke, and added, "It isn't a letter, after all: it's a set of verses."

"Are they in the prisoner's handwriting?" asked another of the jurymen.

"No, they're not," said the White Rabbit, "and that's the queerest thing about it." (The jury all looked puzzled.)

"He must have imitated somebody else's hand," said the King. (The jury all brightened up again.)

"Please your Majesty," said the Knave, "I didn't write it, and they can't prove I did: there's no name signed at the end."

"If you didn't sign it," said the King, "that only makes the matter worse. You *must* have meant some mischief, or else you'd have signed your name like an honest man."

There was a general clapping of hands at this: it was the first really clever thing the King had said that day.

"That *proves* his guilt," said the Queen.

"It proves nothing of the sort!" said Alice. "Why, you don't even know what they're about!"

"Read them," said the King.

The White Rabbit put on his spectacles. "Where shall I begin, please your Majesty?" he asked.

"Begin at the beginning," the King said gravely, "and go on till you come to the end; then stop."

These were the verses the White Rabbit read —

"They told me you had been to her,
And mentioned me to him:
She gave me a good character,
But said I could not swim.

He sent them word I had not gone
(We know it to be true):
If she should push the matter on,
What would become of you?

I gave her one, they gave him two,
You gave us three or more;
They all returned from him to you,

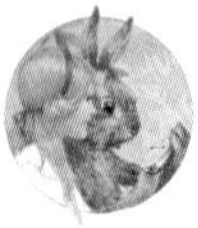

Though they were mine before.

If I or she should chance to be
Involved in this affair,
He trusts to you to set them free,
Exactly as we were.

My notion was that you had been
(Before she had this fit)
An obstacle that came between
Him, and ourselves, and it.

Don't let him know she liked them best,
For this must ever be
A secret, kept from all the rest,
Between yourself and me."

"That's the most important piece of evidence we've heard yet," said the King, rubbing his hands; "so now let the jury—"

"If any one of them can explain it," said Alice (she had grown so large in the last few minutes that she wasn't a bit afraid of interrupting him), "I'll give him sixpence. *I* don't believe there's an atom of meaning in it."

The jury all wrote down on their slates, "*She* doesn't

believe there's an atom of meaning in it," but none of them attempted to explain the paper.

"If there's no meaning in it," said the King, "that saves a world of trouble, you know, as we needn't try to find any. And yet I don't know," he went on, spreading out the verses on his knee, and looking at them with one eye; "I seem to see some meaning in them, after all. '*—said I could not swim—*' you can't swim, can you?" he added, turning to the Knave.

The Knave shook his head sadly. "Do I look like it?" he said. (Which he certainly did not, being made entirely of cardboard.)

"All right, so far," said the King, and he went on muttering over the verses to himself: " '*We know it to be true—*' that's the jury, of course—'I *gave her one, they gave him two—*' why, that must be what he did with the tarts, you know—"

"But, it goes on '*they all returned from him to you,*'" said Alice.

"Why, there they are!" said the King triumphantly, pointing to the tarts on the table. "Nothing can be clearer than *that*. Then again —'*Before she had this fit—*' you never had fits, my dear, I think?" he said to the Queen.

"Never!" said the Queen furiously, throwing an inkstand at the Lizard as she spoke. (The unfortunate little Bill had left off writing on his slate with one finger, as he

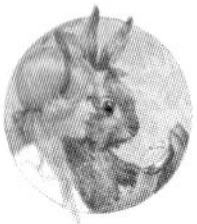

found it made no mark; but he now hastily began again, using the ink, that was trickling down his face, as long as it lasted.)

"Then the words don't *fit* you," said the King, looking round the court with a smile. There was a dead silence.

"It's a pun!" the King added in an offended tone, and everybody laughed.

"Let the Jury consider their verdict," the King said, for about the twentieth time that day.

"No, no!" said the Queen. "Sentence first—verdict afterwards."

"Stuff and nonsense!" said Alice loudly. "The idea of having the sentence first!"

"Hold your tongue!" said the Queen, turning purple.

"I won't!" said Alice.

"Off with her head!" the Queen shouted at the top of her voice. Nobody moved.

"Who cares for you?" said Alice, (she had grown to her full size by this time.) "You're nothing but a pack of cards!"

At this the whole pack rose up into the air, and came flying down upon her: she gave a little scream, half of fright and half of anger, and tried to beat them off, and found herself lying on the bank, with her head in the lap of her sister, who was gently brushing away some dead leaves

that had fluttered down from the trees upon her face.

"Wake up, Alice dear!" said her sister; "Why, what a long sleep you've had!"

"Oh, I've had such a curious dream!" said Alice, and she told her sister, as well as she could remember them, all these strange Adventures of hers that you have just been reading about; and when she had finished, her sister kissed her, and said, "It *was* a curious dream, dear, certainly; but now run in to your tea; it's getting late." So Alice got up and ran off thinking while she ran, as well she might, what a wonderful dream it had been.

But her sister sat still just as she left her, leaning her head on her hand, watching the setting sun, and thinking of little Alice and all her wonderful Adventures, till she too began dreaming after a fashion, and this was her dream—

First, she dreamed of little Alice herself, and once again the tiny hands were clasped upon her knee, and the bright eager eyes were looking up into hers—she could hear the very tones of her voice, and see that queer little toss of her head to keep back the wandering hair that *would* always get into her eyes—and still as she listened, or seemed to listen, the whole place around her became alive with the strange creatures of her little sister's dream.

The long grass rustled at her feet as the White Rabbit

hurried by—the frightened Mouse splashed his way through the neighbouring pool—she could hear the rattle of the teacups as the March Hare and his friends shared their never-ending meal, and the shrill voice of the Queen ordering off her unfortunate guests to execution—once more the pig-baby was sneezing on the Duchess's knee, while plates and dishes crashed around it—once more the shriek of the Gryphon, the squeaking of the Lizard's slate-pencil, and the choking of the suppressed guinea-pigs, filled the air, mixed up with the distant sobs of the miserable Mock Turtle.

So she sat on, with closed eyes, and half believed herself in Wonderland, though she knew she had but to open them again and all would change to dull reality—the grass would be only rustling in the wind, and the pool rippling to the waving of the reeds—the rattling teacups would change to the tinkling sheep-bells, and the Queen's shrill cries to the voice of the shepherd boy—and the sneeze of the baby, the shriek of the Gryphon, and all the other queer noises, would change (she knew) to the confused clamour of the busy farmyard—while the lowing of the cattle in the distance would take the place of the Mock Turtle's heavy sobs.

Lastly, she pictured to herself how this same little sister of hers would, in the after-time, be herself a grown woman; and how she would keep, through all her riper years, the simple and loving heart of her childhood; and how she would gather about her other little children, and make *their* eyes bright and eager with many a strange tale, perhaps even with the dream of Wonderland of long ago; and how she would feel with all their simple sorrows, and find a pleasure in all their simple joys, remembering her own child-life, and the happy summer days.

愛麗絲夢遊仙境

金色的午後，
一切莫不愜意，我們泛著舟；
我們的兩支槳，兩隻小手臂，
不太有技巧地不斷划動槳，
小小的手，
假裝在帶著我們漫遊。

啊，三個殘忍的小東西！這個時刻，
在這樣宜人的天氣下，
央求講一個好聽的故事，
要一個累到連羽毛都吹不動的人來講！
而一個虛弱的聲音，
如何抵得過三張嘴巴的群起攻之？

蠻橫的大女兒毫不猶豫地
發出了命令「快開始」——
比較溫柔的二女兒希望
「故事裡要有瞎掰的內容！」
三女兒每不到一分鐘
就插嘴一次。

不久，她們在一陣安靜中贏了，
愛作夢的孩子，
穿越過一個
不思議的新奇仙境，
與鳥兒和動物們話家常，
有一半的話兒都不假。

當故事乏味了，
當想像力的泉源枯竭了，
只能勉勉強強硬扯時，
那就先到此為止吧，
「下回分曉吧！」「現在已經是下回了！」
這些快活的聲音嚷著。

就這樣，仙境的故事慢慢鋪陳了出來：
慢慢地，一段接著一段，
新奇的事情慢慢地推敲出來，
而現在，大功告成了，
我們掌舵返家，一群快樂的船員，
在落日餘暉的時刻裡。

愛麗絲！上演了一個孩子的故事
一隻溫柔的手，
擱在交織著兒時夢想
的神祕記憶帶上，
就像朝聖者手中枯萎的花圈，
是在遠方摘下來的。

第一章

墜入兔子洞

河岸邊，坐在姊姊身旁沒事可做的愛麗絲，開始感到不耐煩起來。她偷瞄了一、兩次姊姊正在讀的書，書上既沒有插圖，又沒有對話，「居然沒有插圖，也沒有對話，這種書有什麼用啊？」愛麗絲想。

於是，她心裡盤算著（她盡可能集中精神用力去想，因為酷熱的天氣讓她昏昏欲睡，變得遲鈍了），編雛菊花環的樂趣，究竟值不值得讓她起身去摘花呢？這時，突然出現一隻粉紅色眼睛的白兔子，從她身邊跑過。

這種事情本來就沒有什麼值得一提的，因此當愛麗絲聽到兔子自言自語說：「天啊！天啊！我快遲到了！」也不覺得有什麼不尋常的。（稍後，當她再回想起時，才突然想到自己應該感到奇怪才對。可是在當時，一切看起來都是那麼自然。）不過，當兔子從牠背心的口袋裡掏出一隻懷錶，看看時間，再繼續趕路時，

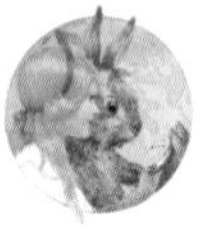

愛麗絲就跳了起來，因為她突然想起自己從沒看過兔子穿背心，更別說口袋裡有懷錶的兔子了。因此在好奇心的驅使下，她越過田野，追著兔子，這時正好及時看到牠跳進樹籬下一個很大的兔子洞裡。

當愛麗絲跟著兔子跳進洞裡時，也沒想說到底要怎麼再從兔子洞裡爬出來。

剛開始，兔子洞是一條直直的長隧道，接著倏然下降，因為路轉得太突然，愛麗絲還來不及反應、停下腳步，就跌進了深井般的洞裡。

如果不是井很深，那就是她往下跌的速度很慢，因為當她往下墜的時候，還有充裕的時間可以觀察四周，並猜想接下來會發生什麼事。剛開始，她往下望，想看清楚自己會掉到哪裡，但下面太暗了，什麼也看不到。然後她看了看井的四周，發現周圍都是碗櫥和書架，掛鉤上吊滿了地圖和畫。在經過其中一個架子的時候，她順手拿了一個果醬瓶，上面標示著「橘子果醬」，但令她失望的是那是個空瓶子。她不敢隨便扔了它，怕會砸傷了下面的人，於是在經過另一個櫥子時，將瓶子放了回去。

ORA

愛麗絲想：「有過這次的經驗以後呢，從樓梯上摔下來就不算什麼了，家人一定會覺得我很勇敢的。不，我才不告訴他們呢，就算我從屋頂摔下來，我也不會把這次的事情說出來。」（從屋頂摔下來倒是真的有可能發生。）

跌啊跌的，要下跌到什麼時候呢？她大聲地對自己說：「不知道我現在已經掉得多深了？我一定已經來到地球的中心點，我看看，應該有四千哩深了吧。」（因為愛麗絲在學校裡學過這類的算術課程，雖然現在不是炫耀知識的好機會，不過反正也沒人聽到，再說做個練習也不錯。）「對，沒錯，大約就是這個深度。可是，不曉得這裡的經緯度是多少？」（愛麗絲並不知道什麼是經緯度，只是覺得這樣的字眼講出來很有水準。）

這時她又開始說道：「照這樣下去，搞不好我會穿過整個地球，在頭朝下走路的人群中出現，那一定很有趣。我想那應該叫做『不相容性』吧。」（她很高興這次沒有人聽到，因為她用的字眼似乎不太正確。）「不過，我應該問問這個國家的名字，也許我該說，這位女士，請問一下，這裡是紐西蘭還是澳洲？」（當她這麼說的時候，還行個屈膝禮，你能想像在空中墜落的情況下還行屈膝禮，你做得到嗎？）「我這麼問，她一定會當我是個無知的小女孩。不，我不會這麼問，或許我能看到某個地方寫著這個國家的名字。」

跌啊跌的，就這樣不斷往下跌。既然無事可做，愛麗絲又開始自言自語起來：「我應該想想黛娜，牠今晚會很想我的。」（黛娜是她的貓。）「希望他們在下午茶時間會記得餵黛娜喝牛奶。親愛的黛娜，真希望你在這裡陪著我，但是空中沒有老鼠可抓，怎麼辦呢？沒關係，你可以抓蝙蝠，牠們和老鼠很像。但我懷疑，貓會吃蝙蝠嗎？」這時候，愛麗絲開始感到愛睏，自言自語也開始像夢囈般顛三倒四：「貓會吃蝙蝠嗎？貓會吃蝙蝠嗎？」有時又變成：「蝙蝠會吃貓嗎？」這兩個問題她自己也回答不上來，她到底是在問哪一個，也不重要。她感覺自己正昏昏睡去，在睡夢中和黛娜牽著手散

步，她誠懇地問黛娜：「黛娜，現在你老實說，你到底有沒有吃過蝙蝠？」突然砰砰的聲響，她摔在樹枝和乾草堆上，整個墜落的過程終於結束。

愛麗絲一點也不覺得痛，立刻就站起來，她抬頭往上望了望，頭頂上一片漆黑。在她前面有另一條長長的通道，而那隻白兔子還在前面趕路。時間不允許愛麗絲稍有耽擱，當兔子轉彎的時候，愛麗絲風也似地追了上去，這時正好聽到牠說：「我的耳朵和鬍鬚，哇，現在已經多晚了呀！」她轉彎，緊跟在兔子身後，但這時兔子已經不見蹤影。她發現自己來到一個低矮的長形大廳，屋頂上吊著一排燈，照亮了整間大廳。

大廳四周都是門，而且門都上了鎖。愛麗絲上前試開每道門，然後傷心地回到了大廳中央，不知道要怎麼離開這個地方。

突然間，她看到一張只有三隻腳的桌子，整張桌子都是用堅硬的玻璃做成，桌子上除了一支小小的金鑰匙之外，什麼都沒有。愛麗絲第一個閃過的念頭，就是這支鑰匙可以打開大廳的其中一扇門。但是，天啊，門鎖都那麼大，而鑰匙那麼小，無論如何都無法打開那些門。然而，當她再度環顧四周，才發現之前沒有注意到的一副矮布簾，布簾後有一道約莫十五吋高的小門，於是她便拿起金鑰匙來試這扇門，令她興奮的是，這支鑰匙可以把門打開！

愛麗絲打開門後，發現了一條和老鼠洞差不多寬的小通道。她跪下身子，向洞裡頭望去，通道那一頭是一個絕美的花園。她多麼希望能離開這個陰暗的大廳，漫步在美麗的花叢和清涼的噴泉間，可是她連頭要伸進去都很困難，可憐的愛麗絲想：「就算我的頭能伸進去，肩膀進不去又有什麼用呢？喔，真希望我可以像望遠鏡

一樣縮起來，只要我知道該怎麼開始，我想我應該做得到才對。」從剛才到現在，發生了這麼多不尋常的事，所以愛麗絲已經開始覺得沒有什麼事是不可能的。

在這個小門前枯等也沒什麼用，愛麗絲只好回到桌子旁，希望能再找到其他的鑰匙，或者至少找到什麼書，上面寫著能讓人像望遠鏡那樣伸縮自如的方法。這次，她看到了桌上有一個小瓶子。（「剛剛並沒有這個瓶子啊。」愛麗絲自言自語說。）瓶口上綁了一張紙條，上面印著兩個漂亮的大字：「喝我」。

沒錯，紙條上是寫著「喝我」兩個字，但聰明的小愛麗絲卻不急著這麼做，她說：「慢著，我得先看看上面是不是有標示著『毒藥』。」她讀過幾篇不錯的兒童短篇故事，故事中有的小孩被燒死，有的被野獸吃掉，不然就是發生一些令人不愉快的事。而發生這些不幸的原因，只是因為沒有記住朋友告誡過的簡單規則：例如，火紅的鐵鉗拿久了會燙傷、小刀割到手通常會流血等，而她不曾忘記過的是，如果喝到標示「毒藥」的東西，身體早晚一定會出問題。

不過，瓶子上並沒有標示「毒藥」這兩個字，所以愛麗絲便冒險嚐了一口，而且發覺還很好喝。（事實上，那是櫻桃餡餅、牛奶蛋糊、鳳梨、烤火雞、太妃糖和熱奶油土司混合的味道。）她一口氣就把整瓶都喝掉了。

「好奇怪的感覺喔，我的身體像望遠鏡一樣地縮小了。」愛麗絲說。

的確，現在她的身體只剩十吋高。她想到這樣的高度正好可以通過小門，進入美麗的花園時，不禁面露喜色。但一開始她等了幾分鐘，看看自己的身體還會不會再縮小，她感到有點擔心。她對著自己說：「如果再照這樣縮小下去，會不會像蠟燭燃燒一樣，越燒越短，不知道那是什麼樣子？」她想像燭火熄滅後蠟燭的樣子，因為她記不得是不是有看過那樣的蠟燭。

過了一會兒，當身體不再縮小時，她決定立刻走進花園。唉，可憐的愛麗絲，當她來到門邊時，才發現忘了帶金鑰匙。她回到桌子那邊想拿鑰匙時，才發現自己已經搆不著鑰匙。透過玻璃，她可以清楚地看到那把鑰匙。她想從桌腳爬上去，但是太滑了，最後因為爬累了，可憐的小愛麗絲就坐在地上哭了起來。

她嚴厲地對自己說：「算了，這樣哭是沒有用的，我勸你馬上離開這裡。」她給自己的建議通常都很不錯。（雖然她很少會照著做。）有時候她會嚴厲地責罵自己，幾乎把自己快罵哭了。還記得有一次，她用力掌了自己一個耳光，原因是她在一場和自己對抗的槌球賽中作弊。這個奇怪的孩子喜歡一人飾演兩個角色。可憐的愛麗絲想：「現在沒用了，連一個像樣的人都扮演不好，假裝成兩個人又有什麼用？」

不久，她的眼光落在桌下的一個小玻璃盒上，她將盒子打開，看見裡面有一塊小蛋糕，上面用葡萄乾整齊地排列出「吃我」兩個字。「好吧，我就把它吃了，如果它能讓我的身體變大，我就可以拿到鑰匙；如果它讓我的身體變小，我就能從門縫鑽過去。不管怎樣，我都能進入花園，管他會發生什麼事！」愛麗絲說。

她吃了一小口蛋糕，然後緊張地對自己說：「會怎麼樣？會怎麼樣？」她把手放到頭頂，去感覺自己是變大還是縮小。讓她驚訝的是，什麼事也沒有發生，她還是和原先一樣大小。當然，吃蛋糕之後身體大小不變，這是很正常的事，但愛麗絲見怪不怪了，所以她期待會有一些不尋常的事發生。平凡無奇的生活，很悶、很枯燥呀。

於是，她繼續吃著，很快就把整個蛋糕都吃掉。

第二章

淚池

「奇怪，越來越奇怪了。」愛麗絲叫道。（她太驚訝了，一時之間竟忘了該怎麼好好說話。）「現在我像大型望遠鏡一樣，身體愈拉愈長了，我的腳呀，再見了。」（因為當她往下看自己的腳時，幾乎已經看不到了，她的腳看起來是那麼遙遠。）「喔，可憐的腳，現在誰來幫你們穿鞋襪呢？親愛的腳，我離你們太遠了，實在是幫不上忙，你們得自己想辦法。不過——我一定要善待它們一點。」愛麗絲心想：「或許它們不能照我的意思來走路了。我來想想看，每年聖誕節我一定要買雙新靴子給它們。」

她繼續在心中盤算該如何對待它們，「這禮物就由送貨員來送好了！」她想：「不過這樣一定很滑稽，送禮物給自己的腳，到時候禮物上的地址會多奇怪啊。

給愛麗絲的右腳先生
地毯鎮
壁爐街
愛你的愛麗絲

天啊，我已經語無倫次了。」

就在此時，她的頭頂到了大廳的屋頂。事實上，她的身高已經超過了九呎。於是，愛麗絲立刻拿起桌上的金鑰匙，衝向通往花園的小門。

可憐的愛麗絲！她竭盡所能地想鑽過去，但即使將身體側躺一邊，也只能用一隻眼睛看到花園，想要鑽過去根本不可能。她坐在地上，又哭了起來。

愛麗絲說：「你應該為自己感到羞恥，像你這麼大的女孩（她絕對有資格這麼說），竟然哭成這樣！我告訴你，別哭了！」但她仍然繼續掉眼淚，還流下了幾加侖的眼淚，直到眼淚在她四周形成了一個大約四吋深的大池塘，將大廳淹了一半高。

過了一會兒，她聽到遠處傳來一陣腳步的啪嗒聲，她急忙擦乾眼淚，看看是誰來了。原來是那隻白兔子回來了。牠穿著華麗的衣服，一手拿著白色的小羊皮手套，一手握著大扇子，匆匆忙忙地向這裡跑來，口中

還喃喃自語道：「喔！公爵夫人，公爵夫人！喔，讓她等了這麼久，希望她不要大發雷霆才好。」此時愛麗絲已經陷入了絕望的谷底，正打算向經過的任何人求助。因此當兔子靠近她時，愛麗絲以低沉而膽怯的聲音說道：「先生，可不可以請你——」話還沒說完，兔子便丟下了白色的小羊皮手套和扇子，逃命似地衝進黑暗中。

愛麗絲撿起了扇子和手套，因為大廳很悶熱，所以她便拿扇子邊搧涼，邊繼續說著：「天啊，天啊！今天發生的事怎麼都那麼奇怪！昨天一切都還很正常啊，難道是昨晚我身上發生了什麼變化嗎？讓我想想看，今天早上起床的時候，我還是原來的我嗎？我想，我記得感覺不太一樣了。如果我已經不是原來的我，那麼接下來的問題是，在這個世界的我又是誰呢？唉，這真是個難解的謎啊！」然後她開始想起和她同年齡的孩子，想想她自己是不是變成了他們其中的一個。

她說：「我確定我不是艾達，她有長長的鬈髮，而我沒有。我確定我也不是梅寶，我知識這麼淵博，而她這麼無知！何況她是她，我是我。喔，天啊，這一切實在是太令人困惑了。這樣吧，我來看看以前學過的東西是不是還記得：四乘五是十二，四乘六是十三，四乘七是——完了，像這樣的速度我永遠也背不到二十！算了，九九乘法不會又不代表什麼。我來試試地理好了，倫敦是巴黎的首都，巴黎是羅馬的首都，而羅馬是——不對，一定都錯了，我一定是變成梅寶了！我再背段課文試試，『小小的——是如何——』」當她在背課文時，還把手交叉放在膝蓋上，彷彿在課堂上背書似的。只是她的聲音變得粗糙而怪異，背誦出來的字句也和平常不太相同：

小小的鱷魚是如何
擦亮自己的尾巴，
然後將尼羅河的水，
潑在每片金色的鱗片上！

看牠笑得多開心，
出手多凌厲，
張開優雅微笑的大嘴，
迎接魚兒游進來！

可憐的愛麗絲，再度噙著淚水，說道：「我敢說我背錯了，我一定變成梅寶了，我可能要住在這個狹窄難受的地方了，身旁又沒有玩具可以玩，喔！還有那麼多功課要做！不，我決定了，如果我是梅寶的話，我就永遠待在這裡好了，就算他們把頭伸進來對我說：『親愛的，出來吧！』我也只會抬頭看一眼，然後說：『你們得先說出我是誰？除非你們先說出人名來，我要是想當那個人，我就出來；如果我不想，我就要一直待在這裡，直到你們說我是另一個人為止。』但是，老天爺啊！」愛麗絲突然哭了起來，「真希望有人探頭來對我說話，我討厭一個人孤伶伶地待在這裡！」

她一邊說，一邊往下看著自己的手，她驚訝地發現，她說話時，手上正戴著那隻兔子的小白羊皮手套。「我怎麼做到的？一定是我的身體又變小了。」她想。她站起來，走到桌子旁量身高，才發現，正如她所猜想

的，她只剩兩呎高了，而且正迅速地縮小中。她很快發現這是因為她手中握的扇子所造成的。於是，她趕緊丟下，及時避免了一直縮小到消失不見。

「剛才真是好險！」愛麗絲說道，雖然被剛才突然的改變嚇到，但還是很高興自己還存在著。「現在向花園出發吧！」她全速向小門衝過去，不過，哎喲，小門又關上了，而那支金鑰匙仍放在玻璃桌上。「情況變得更慘了，我變得比之前更小了，我還沒有這麼小過，我慘兮兮了，真的！」這可憐的孩子想。

正在說話的時候，她滑了一跤，摔到一個深及下巴的鹹水池裡。她第一個念頭是，自己可能跌進海裡了。她對自己說：「萬一是這樣的話，我就可以坐火車回家了。」（愛麗絲一輩子就只去過海邊一次，她的結論是，不管去英國的哪一個海岸，都可以在海邊看到很多淋浴間、用木鏟挖沙的一些小孩們、一整排的出租公寓，還有公寓後面的鐵路。）然而沒多久，她發現，所

謂的海，其實是她剛才有九呎高時所哭成的淚池。

「要是我剛才沒哭那麼厲害就好了！」愛麗絲一邊說，一邊四處游著，尋找出口。「我想這就是報應吧，被自己的眼淚淹死，這種死法還真奇怪！反正今天發生的事情都很奇怪。」

就在這時，她聽到不遠處有個東西撲通一聲掉進水裡，於是她朝發出聲音的地方游去，一探究竟。一開始，她以為那不是海象就是河馬，但之後她忽然想起自己現在變得這麼小，很快她就發現，原來只是一隻老鼠像她一樣不小心滑進淚池了。

愛麗絲想：「現在跟老鼠講話不知道能不能溝通？今天在這裡發生的事都那麼不尋常，所以老鼠會講話應該也很有可能的。不管怎樣，試一試也無妨。」因此，她開始對老鼠說：「喂，老鼠，你知道要怎麼離開這個水池嗎？我已經游得很累了。喂，老鼠！」（愛麗絲認為，這樣對老鼠說話應該沒錯。雖然她以前沒和老鼠說過話，但她記得曾看過哥哥的拉丁文法書上寫著『一隻老鼠——一隻老鼠的——對一隻老鼠——一隻老鼠——喔，老鼠！』）老鼠不發一語，只是打量著她，好像在對她眨著小眼睛。

愛麗絲想：「搞不好牠聽不懂英文，我敢說牠一定是隻法國老鼠，跟著征服者威廉一起過來的。」（愛麗絲所知的歷史有限，她根本不清楚什麼事情發生在什麼時代。）所以她開始用法文說：「我的貓在哪裡？」這是她在法文課本裡所學到的第一個句子，只見這隻老鼠突然躍出水面，像是嚇得全身打哆嗦。「喔，對不起！」愛麗絲趕緊叫道，怕自己刺激到了這隻可憐的動物，「我差點忘了，你不喜歡貓。」

「我不喜歡貓，如果你是我，你會喜歡貓嗎？」老鼠用尖銳而激動的聲音叫道。

愛麗絲用和緩的語氣說：「應該不會吧。你別生氣嘛，不過我希望你可以見見我的貓咪黛娜，只要你看到

牠，你就會喜歡上貓的，牠是一個安靜的小寶貝。」愛麗絲一邊在池水中懶散地游著，一邊自言自語地說：「牠會坐在火爐旁，舒服地發出呼嚕呼嚕的聲音，舔自己的腳掌，用腳掌洗臉。牠的毛摸起來很舒服，還有牠很會抓老鼠──喔，對不起！」愛麗絲再度叫道，因為這次老鼠全身的毛都豎立起來，她感覺到這次是真的冒犯到牠了。「如果你不喜歡的話，我們就不要談這個話題了。」

「我們不談了。」老鼠叫道。牠從頭到尾巴都在顫抖。「講得好像我很喜歡這個話題似的，我們家族一向恨透了貓這種噁心、下流、鄙俗的東西，別讓我再聽到這個字了。」

「不會了，真的！」愛麗絲很快改變話題：「你──你喜歡──喜歡狗嗎？」老鼠沒反應，愛麗絲於是繼續急切地說：「我想跟你介紹我們家附近一隻很不錯的小狗，牠是一隻眼睛炯炯有神的獵狗，有棕色的長鬈毛！如果你把東西丟出去，牠會跑去接，還有牠會用後腳站立，像在祈求食物那樣。除了這些，牠還會很多把戲，我連其中的一半都記不得。牠是一位農夫養的，他說這隻狗很好用，至少值一百英鎊！農夫說牠也很會抓老鼠

——喔，天啊！」愛麗絲帶著歉意的語調說：「恐怕我又冒犯牠了！」因為老鼠正拚命地游離她的身旁，池水一陣騷動。

因此她在牠身後輕聲叫道：「親愛的老鼠，你回來吧，如果你不喜歡，我們就不要再談貓和狗了！」老鼠聽到這些話，才回過頭緩慢地游向她，可是牠的臉仍十分蒼白（愛麗絲認為牠太激動了）。老鼠用低沉而顫抖的聲音說：「我們游到岸邊，我來慢慢告訴你我過去的歷史，這樣你就能了解我為什麼那麼痛恨貓和狗了。」

現在離開正是時候，因為池子裡陸續有鳥和動物掉進來，開始有些擁擠了。現在池子裡有鴨子、渡渡鳥、小鸚鵡、小飛鷹和各種奇怪的動物。愛麗絲便領著這一群動物，向岸邊游去。

第三章

高加斯會議賽跑和長篇故事

聚集在岸邊的動物都長得很奇怪，鳥兒們的羽毛凌亂不堪，毛緊貼在身上。大家渾身都溼透了，感到煩躁、不舒服。

首先要解決的問題，當然是如何把身體弄乾。大家開會，商量了一下這個問題。幾分鐘後，愛麗絲發現自己已經可以熟稔地和牠們交談，彼此就像熟識一樣。的確，愛麗絲和鸚鵡爭執了好一會兒，最後鸚鵡生氣了，只說了一句：「我的年紀比你大，知道的比你多。」由於不知道鸚鵡的年紀到底有多大，所以愛麗絲說什麼也不肯讓步，既然鸚鵡拒絕透露自己的年齡，他們之間就不再說話了。

最後，他們當中看起來較具權威的老鼠說話了：「你們都坐下，聽我說！我有辦法讓你們趕快把身體弄乾！」牠們立刻坐下來，圍了一個大圈，把老鼠圍在中間。愛麗絲殷切地看著牠，因為她知道，如果再不趕快把身體弄乾的話，一定會得重感冒的。

「咳！咳！」老鼠鄭重其事地說道：「你們準備好了嗎？這是我所知道最乾燥†的事了，請大家安靜！『征服者威廉受到教皇的支持，渴望領導者的英國子民很快就臣服，因為近年來，他們都習慣了被侵占和征服。艾德溫和摩卡，邁西亞和諾桑比亞的伯爵——』」

「呃！」鸚鵡顫抖了一下，叫出聲音。

「對不起！剛才是你在說話嗎？」老鼠皺起眉頭，但仍有禮貌地說。

「不，我沒有！」鸚鵡趕緊回答。

老鼠說：「我還以為你說了什麼，我要繼續說了，『艾德溫和摩卡，邁西亞和諾桑比亞的伯爵也支持威廉，就連愛國的坎特伯里大主教史丁格，也發現它是個明智之舉——』」

「發現什麼？」鴨子問。

老鼠用憤怒的語氣回答：「發現『它』，你們當然應該知道『它』是什麼意思。」

鴨子說：「我當然知道『它』是什麼意思，當我發現了什麼東西的時候，『它』通常是指一隻青蛙或小蟲，問題是大主教究竟發現了什麼？」

老鼠不理會這個問題，很快地繼續說下去：「『發

† dry 亦有「枯燥」之意，雙關語。

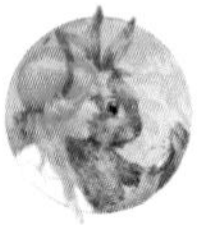

現和艾德格·亞瑟林一起去晉見威廉王，並授與他皇冠是明智之舉。剛開始，威廉王的行為還算溫和，但是那些傲慢的諾曼第人──』親愛的，你們現在覺得怎麼樣？」老鼠繼續說，一面把頭轉向愛麗絲。

愛麗絲用憂心的口吻說：「還是和之前一樣濕啊！這好像一點也不能把我弄乾。」

渡渡鳥站起來，嚴肅地說：「我提議休會，立刻採取有效的補救措施──」

小飛鷹說：「請說英語！你剛剛說了一長串，我一個字也聽不懂，我想你自己也不懂吧！」小飛鷹低下頭吃吃地偷笑，其他的鳥也笑出聲音來。

「我的意思是，把我們身體弄乾最好的方法，就是來個高加斯會議賽跑。」渡渡鳥生氣地說。

「什麼是高加斯會議賽跑？」愛麗絲問。她並不是真的想知道，而是渡渡鳥故意停頓了一下，好像期待有人會發問，可是看起來沒有人要發問的樣子。

渡渡鳥說：「這個嘛，要解釋這個問題最好的方法，就是實際去做。」（你可能會想在冬天裡嘗試，所以我就告訴你渡渡鳥是如何辦到的。）

牠先在地上畫出一個類似圓形的跑道，（渡渡鳥說：「跑道圓不圓，不重要。」）然後牠將所有的動物安排

在跑道上，並沒有什麼「一、二、三，開始」的程序，牠們高興什麼時候起跑或停止都可以，所以很難說比賽什麼時候結束。然而，當牠們大約跑了半小時之後，身體就都乾了。渡渡鳥突然喊道：「比賽結束！」大夥一窩蜂地擠向渡渡鳥，喘著氣問：「誰贏了？」

這個問題渡渡鳥一時也答不上來，牠坐著沉吟了好一會兒，用一隻手指抵住前額（這是在莎士比亞的照片中最常見的姿勢）。大家在沉默中靜待牠的答案，最後渡渡鳥說：「大家都贏了，大家都有獎品！」

「那誰來提供獎品？」大家異口同聲說道。

「這個嘛——當然是她囉。」渡渡鳥用一根手指指向愛麗絲說。於是，所有的動物便擠向愛麗絲，混亂地圍著她叫嚷：「獎品！獎品！」

愛麗絲不知道怎麼辦才好，她在不知所措中從口袋裡摸出了一盒糖果（還好鹹水沒有滲進盒子裡），她把糖果發下去當作獎品，盒中的糖剛好夠大家各發一個。

「可是她自己應該也有獎品才對。」老鼠說。

渡渡鳥非常認真地回答：「那當然，你口袋裡還有什麼東西？」牠邊說，邊把頭轉向愛麗絲。

「只剩下一支打毛線的頂針了。」愛麗絲傷心地說。

「把它拿出來。」渡渡鳥說。

大家又再度圍著她，渡渡鳥很隆重地將頂針頒給愛麗絲，說：「這隻高雅的頂針，請您笑納。」說完之後，全場一陣歡呼聲。

愛麗絲覺得這整件事情真荒謬，但看到大家認真的樣子，就不敢笑出來。她想不出要講什麼致詞，便簡單地鞠個躬，接過頂針，讓自己看起來莊重嚴肅一點。

接下來吃糖果的時候，又引起了一陣騷動和混亂。體型大的鳥嫌不能吃，體型小的鳥又噎到，還得有人替牠們拍拍背。不管怎樣，大家最後總算吃完了。於是這群動物又圍成一圈坐下來，要老鼠再說故事給牠們聽。

愛麗絲說：「你答應過我，要跟我說你以前的事，你為什麼那麼討厭——ㄇ和ㄍ呢？」她輕聲地加了一句，有點怕會再刺激到牠。

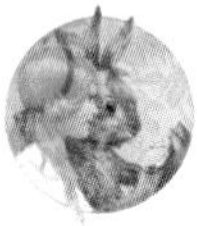

「我的故事（tale）可說是又長又悲哀啊！」老鼠轉向愛麗絲，嘆了一口氣說。

愛麗絲充滿疑惑地往老鼠的尾巴（tail）†看去，說道：「它當然是很長囉，但你怎麼會說它悲哀呢？」當老鼠正講著牠的事情時，愛麗絲仍不斷猜疑著這個問題，所以整個故事在她聽起來就像這樣†：

「費瑞對一隻在酒館裡偶
遇的老鼠說：『我們一
起去法院吧，我要控告你，
來吧，決不撤訴。我們
一定要開庭
一下，因
為我今天早上實
在閒得發慌。』老鼠
對癩皮狗費瑞說：『親
愛的先生，我們這
樣開個庭，沒有陪
審團，沒有法官，瞎
搞而已嘛。』『我
來當法官、當陪
審團好啦。』狡
猾的老費瑞說：
『我來審判整個
訴訟，判
你個死
刑。』」

† tale 和 tail 同音
† 文字故意排成尾巴的樣子

「你根本沒在注意聽嘛！你到底在想什麼？」老鼠嚴厲地對愛麗絲說。

愛麗絲低聲下氣地說：「對不起，你是不是講到第五節了？」

「還沒！（not）」老鼠生氣而嚴厲地叫道。

「『結』（knot）？†」愛麗絲說。她一臉憂心，總希望自己能幫得上忙。「喔，我來幫你把結打開吧！」

「我才不要做那種事，你那些毫無意義的話已經侮辱到我了！」老鼠說完，站起來準備掉頭走開。

可憐的愛麗絲乞求道：「我不是故意的，你不要這麼容易生氣嘛！」

老鼠沒有說什麼，發出了憤怒的低吼。

「請你回來把故事說完！」愛麗絲在牠身後大喊，其他動物也一起喊道：「對啊，請你回來！」可是老鼠只是不耐煩地搖搖頭，加快腳步。

當老鼠消失不見時，鸚鵡嘆了一口氣說：「真可惜，牠不肯留下來！」一隻老螃蟹趁機對女兒進行機會教育：「女兒啊，記住這個教訓，千萬不要輕易動怒！」小螃蟹有些不耐煩地說：「媽，別說了，你講的話足夠考驗一隻牡蠣的耐性了！」

† not 和 knot 同音

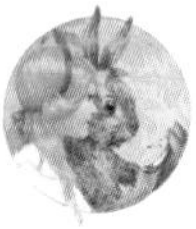

愛麗絲大聲地說：「我家的黛娜要是在就好了，她一下子就能把老鼠叼回來！」愛麗絲大聲地說，沒有特別針對誰說。

「請恕我冒昧問一下，誰是黛娜？」鸚鵡說道。

愛麗絲很喜歡談她的寵物，便熱切地回答：「黛娜是我的貓，她捉老鼠的技巧超乎想像得快！啊，真希望你能看到牠追逐鳥的樣子！她一看到小鳥，就會立刻把牠吃掉！」

這番話在動物群裡引起不小的騷動，有些鳥立刻逃離開。一隻老喜鵲開始仔細整理身上的羽毛，說道：「我真的該回家了，晚上的空氣對我的喉嚨不太好！」一隻金絲雀顫抖著聲音對小孩們喊道：「親愛的，走了！上床的時間到了！」所有的動物紛紛找各種不同的藉口離去，不一會兒，就只剩愛麗絲一個人。

愛麗絲鬱鬱寡歡地說：「剛才要是沒提到黛娜就好了，在這裡好像沒人喜歡她，不過我確定她是天底下最好的貓！喔，親愛的黛娜！不知道我還能不能再看到你！」說到這裡，可憐的愛麗絲又哭了起來，她覺得很孤單、很沮喪。過了一會兒，遠處又傳來細碎的腳步聲，她渴切地向遠方看去，有點希望是老鼠改變心意，回來繼續講未竟的故事。

第四章

白兔派小比爾進屋子

原來是白兔子慢慢踱著大步走回來了，牠焦慮地四下張望，好像丟掉了什麼東西似的，愛麗絲聽到牠嘴裡喃喃唸道：「公爵夫人！公爵夫人！喔，我親愛的爪子！喔，我的毛，我的鬍子！她一定會把我處死的，這就像雪貂一定是雪貂那樣的確定。奇怪，我到底把它們丟到哪裡了去？」愛麗絲馬上就猜到牠一定是在找那支扇子和那雙白色的小羊皮手套，於是她好心地開始幫忙尋找，但到處都找不到。自從她掉進淚池後，一切好像都變了：大廳、玻璃桌、小門都不見了。

白兔子很快留意到愛麗絲在替牠找東西，便很生氣地對她叫道：「喂，瑪莉安，你跑來這裡做什麼？你現在趕緊回家幫我拿一支扇子和一雙手套過來！快點，現在就去！」愛麗絲很害怕，便立刻朝兔子所指的方向跑去，也沒向兔子解釋牠認錯人了。

她邊跑邊對自己說：「牠一定以為我是牠的佣人，如果牠發現我是誰，一定會很訝異的。我最好替牠把扇子和手套拿過來——要是我找得到的話。」話還沒說完，她就來到一間乾淨的小屋子前，只見門上掛著一塊亮澄澄的銅牌，上面刻著「小白兔」三個字。她門也沒敲，就衝上二樓，很怕碰到真正的瑪莉安，讓自己在還沒找到手套和扇子之前就被趕出門。

愛麗絲自言自語說：「真奇怪，我竟然受白兔子的差遣！我想，搞不好下次我會變成黛娜的僕人！」她開始想像可能會發生的情景：「『愛麗絲小姐，請直接過來，準備好去跑腿一下！』『好的，奶媽，我馬上就來！不過，我得在黛娜回來之前，先幫看著老鼠窩，不讓老鼠跑出來。』」愛麗絲繼續說：「但我想，如果黛娜開始在家這樣使喚人，他們一定會喝止黛娜的！」

就在這時候，她來到了一個整齊的小房間，房裡的一扇窗戶旁有個小桌子，（正如她所期望的）上面放著一支扇子和兩、三雙小白羊皮手套。她拿起扇子和一雙手套正準備離開房間的時候，突然在鏡子旁邊看到一個小瓶子。這一次，瓶子上沒有任何標籤寫著「喝我」，但愛麗絲還是打開瓶蓋，張口就喝。她對自己說：「只要我吃什麼或喝什麼，就會有好玩的事情發生，這瓶喝下去不知道會怎麼樣？希望可以讓我又變大一點，我現在這麼小，感覺很膩了！」

這瓶飲料真的應驗了她的期望，甚至比她預期的還要快，半瓶都還沒喝完，頭就已經頂到天花板了。她還必須彎下腰來，以免脖子被折斷。她趕緊把瓶子丟向一旁，對著自己說：「這樣夠了，希望我不要再長高了，不然連大門都出不去，如果剛才沒喝那麼多就好了！」

唉呀！現在說這個已經太遲了！她不斷地長大，身體越變越大，很快地，她就不得不跪在地上，又過了一會兒，房裡甚至已經沒有多餘的空間了。她只好側躺著，用手肘頂住門，再把另一隻手彎起來，蜷在頭上。但她仍繼續在長大，最後只好把一隻手伸出窗外，一隻腳放進煙囪裡。她喃喃自語說：「再長大下去，我就沒地方可以伸了，不知道我會變成什麼樣子？」

所幸，這神奇的小瓶子這時的功效已經全部發揮完了，她停止了變大。不過，愛麗絲仍覺得很難受，看來她根本無法再離開這個房間了，難怪她感到很煩悶。

可憐的愛麗絲心想：「在家裡舒服多了，至少身體不會一下變大、一下變小，也不會被老鼠和兔子使喚來、使喚去的，真希望當初沒有跳進兔子洞裡——不過——不過——這樣的生活真是詭異！以前我讀童話故事

時，喜歡幻想那些不可能發生的事，而現在居然真的碰上這種事了！我應該把發生在我身上的怪事寫成一本書，等我長大了，我就要自己來寫。不過，我現在就已經長大了呀。」她有點難過地加了一句：「起碼這裡已經沒有空間再讓我長大了。」

愛麗絲心想：「那我以後是不是就不會再長大了？這倒是好事，至少我不會變成老女人，不過這樣我就要一直做功課了，我討厭做功課！」

愛麗絲回答自己的問題說：「愛麗絲，你這個小傻瓜，你怎麼可能在這裡做功課呢？這裡都快塞不下你了，哪還有地方讓你放課本？」

就這樣，愛麗絲繼續自問自答，開始演雙簧。幾分鐘後，她聽到外面傳來聲音，便停下來聽聽到底是誰。

「瑪莉安！瑪莉安！」外面的聲音叫道：「馬上把我的手套拿下來。」接著，樓梯傳來一陣腳步聲。愛麗絲知道兔子回來找她了，她嚇得全身發抖，整個屋子都搖晃了起來。她忘了自己比兔子還大上一千倍，根本犯不著害怕了。

這時兔子已經來到房門前，打算開門進來，但這扇門是向房裡開的，而愛麗絲的手肘正好壓在門上，兔子無法把門推開。愛麗絲聽到牠自言自語地說：「沒關係，我繞一圈，從後面的窗戶進去。」

「你進不來的！」愛麗絲想。她一邊等著，直到當她聽到兔子來到窗戶邊時，便突然把手伸出窗外，在空中抓了一下，但什麼也沒抓著。不過她聽到了一聲尖叫，然後是東西落地和玻璃破碎的聲音。聽到這些聲音，她推斷兔子可能是掉進類似種黃瓜的玻璃溫室裡。

接著，傳來了氣呼呼的聲音——那是白兔的聲音——「派特！派特！你在哪裡？」一個愛麗絲很陌生的聲音回答說：「主人，我在這裡！我在挖蘋果！」

兔子生氣地說：「挖蘋果？馬上給我過來，把我拉出來！」（又是一陣玻璃破碎的聲音。）

「派特，你說，窗戶裡面那個是什麼東西？」

「主人，那是一隻手！」（他的咬字不太清楚，聽起來有些像「熟」。）

「你這個白癡，什麼手？你有看過這麼大隻的手、把窗戶都塞滿了的嗎？」

「主人，你說的沒錯，但那真的是一隻手。」

「好啦，不管它是什麼，擋在那裡很礙事，你過去把它移開！」

說完話後，四周接著安靜了一陣子，愛麗絲只偶爾聽到輕聲的低語：「主人，我也不喜歡那隻手！不喜歡！不喜歡！」「照我的話去做就對了，你這個懦夫！」愛麗絲最後又伸出手在空中抓了一下，這次傳來了兩個尖叫聲，還有更多的玻璃碎片聲。「外面一定有很多的黃瓜溫室。」愛麗絲心想：「不知道牠們接下來又想做什麼？把我從窗戶拉出來嗎？只希望牠們拉得動，我也不想再待在這裡！」

愛麗絲等了一段時間，沒有聽到任何聲音。最後，

她聽到一陣隆隆的車輪聲，還有一群人七嘴八舌的說話聲：「其他的梯子在哪裡？——我只帶了一個，比爾那裡還有一個。——比爾，去把梯子搬過來這裡！——這裡，架在這個角落。——不對，你要先把它們綁在一起，這樣連一半的高度都不到。——喔，這樣就夠了啦，別挑剔了！——比爾，這裡！抓住這條繩子。——屋頂能承受重量嗎？——小心那塊快鬆掉的石綿瓦。——喔，快掉下來了！小心你們的頭！（砰的一聲）誰搞的鬼啊？——我想大概是比爾吧。——誰要從煙囪爬下去？——不，我不要！你去！——那我也不要！——比爾，你下去。——比爾，聽到沒？主人叫你從煙囪爬下去！」

愛麗絲自言自語說：「喔，難道比爾非得下來不可嗎？牠們幹嘛什麼事都推給比爾？我才不要像比爾那樣！這個壁爐真的是太窄了，但我想我的腳應該還有空間可以踢一下！」

W-RABBIT

她盡量把腳縮在煙囪下方，在那邊等著，這時她聽到一個小動物從煙囪上面，窸窸窣窣地向她爬過來（到底是什麼動物，她聽不出來。）她對自己說：「比爾來了。」然後她很快地踢了腳，靜待接下來的反應。

首先，她聽到大家齊聲喊道：「比爾飛出去了！」然後是兔子的聲音：「你們在樹籬邊的，把比爾接住！」接著是一陣沉寂，然後又聽到大家七嘴八舌地說：「把牠的頭抬高——把白蘭地拿過來——別噎死牠了——你覺得怎麼樣了，老傢伙？——告訴我們發生了什麼事？」

最後，傳來一陣微弱的嘎吱聲。（「那是比爾吧。」愛麗絲想。）「噢，我什麼也不知道。夠了，謝謝你，我現在覺得好多了，可是我頭腦還是一片混亂，沒辦法告訴你們什麼，我只知道，有個像從玩偶盒跳出來的東西衝向我，然後我就像火箭般飛上天了！」

其他人說：「對啊，老傢伙，你剛才就像火箭一樣沖上天！」

「我們一定要放火把房子燒了！」兔子說道。愛麗絲盡全力大叫一聲說：「如果你們敢，我就叫黛娜咬死你們！」

突然，四周一片安靜，愛麗絲心想：「不曉得接下來牠們又要做什麼？如果牠們聰明點，就應該先把房子拆掉。」過了一、兩分鐘，牠們又開始動了起來。愛麗絲聽到小白兔說：「第一次裝滿一台車就好了。」

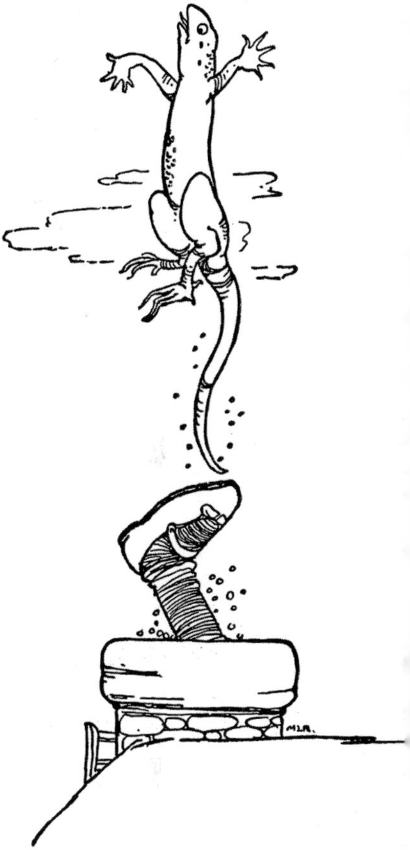

愛麗絲想：「裝滿一車什麼東西啊？」不過，她並沒有遲疑很久，因為一下子，就有一堆鵝卵石像雨點般、劈哩啪啦地從窗戶打進來，有些還打到她臉上。她對自己說：「我得加以制止。」她大叫：「你們最好趕快停止！」接著又是一陣安靜。

愛麗絲驚訝地發現，那些鵝卵石掉到地上後，都變成了一塊塊的小蛋糕。一個念頭閃過她的腦子裡，她想：「我如果吃了這些蛋糕，搞不好身體又會改變大小。現在我的身體不可能變得更大了，所以這些蛋糕應該會讓我變小吧。」

於是，她吃了一些蛋糕，然後欣喜地發現自己的身體迅速地縮小了。當她的身體縮到可以通過房門時，便立刻衝了出去，接著只見一群小動物和鳥在外面等著。可憐的蜥蜴比爾也在動物群中，由兩隻天竺鼠攙扶著，牠們正在餵蜥蜴喝一瓶東西。愛麗絲一出現，大家馬上衝向她。愛麗絲於是沒命地奔逃，一會兒，就平安地逃進濃密的森林裡。

愛麗絲在森林裡閒逛著，她對自己說：「現在，我要做的第一件事，是再恢復到我真正的大小。第二件事呢，我要找到通往美麗花園的路。我想這是最好的做法了。」

這個計畫聽起來的確很不錯，清楚又簡單，唯一的困難就是她不知道該如何著手進行。她焦慮地在樹林中四處張望，這時頭頂上突然傳來一陣尖銳的狗叫聲，她連忙抬頭往上望。

一隻巨大的小狗睜著又圓又大的眼睛看著她。小狗輕輕伸出一隻腳掌，想碰觸愛麗絲，愛麗絲只好哄著牠說：「可憐的小東西！」她努力對牠吹出口哨，但心裡其實始終很害怕，心想牠要是肚子餓了，那不管怎麼哄牠，自己都有可能被吃掉。

PEPPERMINT.

她幾乎是無意識地撿起一根樹枝，向小狗伸過去。沒想到小狗一看見樹枝就跳了起來，興奮地汪汪叫，然後撲向樹枝，一副想咬樹枝的樣子。愛麗絲躲在大薊樹叢後，以免被小狗踩到。但她出現在樹叢的另一端時，小狗又一次衝向樹枝，想抓住樹枝，結果因為衝得太快，跌了個四腳朝天。愛麗絲覺得自己好像在跟一匹拖貨車的馬玩，隨時有被踩死的可能，於是她開始繞著薊樹叢跑。小狗先是向樹枝攻擊了一會兒，往前猛撲，然後再躲得遠遠的，不時沙啞地狂吠。最後玩累了，便在另一頭坐下來，半閉著大眼睛，伸出舌頭，氣喘吁吁。

這似乎是愛麗絲逃跑的最好機會，於是她立刻向外衝出去，拚命地跑，直到累癱了，喘不過氣為止。而遠處傳來的狗叫聲，也越來越微弱。

「這隻狗還真可愛！」愛麗絲靠在毛莨上歇息，一邊用毛莨的葉子搧涼，一邊自言自語說：「我的身體要是恢復了正常的大小，我應該會很喜歡教牠玩很多把戲，！喔，天啊！我差一點忘了要讓自己的身體變大了！我看看，該怎麼做才好？應該要吃什麼或喝什麼的，不過問題是，要吃什麼、喝什麼呢？」

KMR

最大的問題是要吃什麼、喝什麼？愛麗絲環顧四周的花草，都沒有發現任何看起來可以吃、可以喝的東西。不過她身邊有一朵和她一樣高的蘑菇，愛麗絲看看蘑菇的下面、兩側和後面，什麼都沒看到。這時，她想到她應該也要看看蘑菇的上面才對。

愛麗絲踮起腳尖，從蘑菇的邊緣瞧了瞧，忽然發現一條巨大的藍色毛毛蟲。毛毛蟲雙手交叉在胸前，正悠閒地坐在蘑菇上抽著水煙斗，沒注意到她或任何東西。

第五章

毛毛蟲的忠告

愛麗絲和毛毛蟲在沉默中大眼瞪小眼，互相凝視了好一段時間。最後，毛毛蟲終於從嘴裡拿出水煙斗來，沒精打采、愛睏地問愛麗絲：

「你是誰？」毛毛蟲問。

這不是一句能打開話題的開場白。愛麗絲有些羞怯地回答：「先生，我——我現在還不知道，至少今天早上起床時，我還知道我是誰，但之後我變了好幾次。」

毛毛蟲冷冷地說：「什麼意思？解釋一下！」

「先生，恐怕不能，因為我不是我自己。」愛麗絲說。

「不懂。」毛毛蟲說。

愛麗絲很有禮貌地說：「我想我也沒辦法說得清楚，首先，我自己也不曉得究竟是怎麼一回事。而且我這樣一天之內，忽大忽小變了好幾次，腦筋已經有點糊塗了。」

「不會的。」毛毛蟲說。

愛麗絲說：「噢，那大概是因為你現在還沒有體驗到吧，但等你變成蛹、再變成蝴蝶時——總有這麼一天，對吧——到時候你也會覺得怪怪的，不是嗎？」

「我才不會。」毛毛蟲說。

「噢，那大概是你的感覺和我不一樣吧，但對我而言，我覺得很困惑。」愛麗絲說。

毛毛蟲輕蔑地說：「你！你到底是誰？」

他們的對話又回到原點。愛麗絲對毛毛蟲剛才那種一字半句的回答，感到有點生氣。她挺起胸膛，嚴肅地對毛毛蟲說：「我想你應該先告訴我你是誰才對。」

「為什麼？」毛毛蟲說。

又是一個令人困惑的問題，愛麗絲想不出有什麼比較好的理由，而毛毛蟲看起來又不太高興的樣子，於是她便掉頭離開。

「回來！」毛毛蟲在她身後叫道：「我有重要的事要跟你說！」

這句話聽起來還有點吸引力，於是愛麗絲轉頭走回來。

「控制你的脾氣。」毛毛蟲說。

「你就要告訴我這些嗎？」愛麗絲盡量壓抑住怒氣說。

「不是。」毛毛蟲說。

愛麗絲心想，既然也沒什麼事好做，不妨就聽聽看牠要說什麼吧，搞不好會說出什麼還值得聽的事情。然而，在接下來的幾分鐘，毛毛蟲只顧抽著煙，一句話也沒說。最後，牠把交叉的手放下來，再將水煙斗從嘴裡拿開，說：「那你是認為你變了，是嗎？」

「沒錯，先生，我已經不太能記住事情，而且無法一直維持同樣的大小，即使只是十分鐘。」愛麗絲回答。

「你記不得什麼事？」毛毛蟲問。

「噢，我想把《忙碌的小蜜蜂》背出來，但背出的內容卻完全走樣。」愛麗絲很沮喪地回答。

「你背《威廉老爹》看看。」毛毛蟲說。

愛麗絲雙手交叉，開始背了起來：

「『您老了，威廉老爹。』年輕人說道。
『您白髮蒼蒼，
卻還一直喜歡倒立——
您一把年紀了，這樣好嗎？』

威廉老爹回答兒子說：『我年輕時，
還擔心倒立會傷大腦，
不過現在，我知道我並沒有大腦，
所以就倒立啊又倒立。』

年輕人說：『我說了，您老了。
身材變得這麼胖，
進門時還可以翻觔斗，
天啊，怎麼辦到的？』

這個有智慧的老人搖搖滿頭白髮說：『我年輕時，
都用這種軟膏，
保持手腳柔軟——一盒一先令——
我可以賣你兩盒嗎？』

年輕人說：『您老了，齒牙鬆動，
咬不動比板油還硬的東西了。
可是，您吃鵝的時候，竟連骨頭和和鵝嘴一起吃下去——
天啊，您是怎麼辦到的？』

他的父親說：『我年輕時，常上法院，
每個案件都會拿來和老婆爭論，
肌肉就變壯了，讓嘴巴的咬合變得很有力，
之後一生都這樣。』

年輕人說：『您老了，
眼睛也該花了，
但是您還能將鰻魚頂在鼻尖上，
是什麼讓您身手這麼靈活的？』

他的父親說：『我已經回答了你三個問題，
別裝模作樣了，
你以為我喜歡整天聽這些廢話嗎？
快滾吧，不然就把你踢下樓去！』」

「你背錯了。」毛毛蟲說。

愛麗絲膽怯地說：「沒有完全正確，有些字背錯了。」

「從頭到尾都背錯了。」毛毛蟲很肯定地說。接著一陣沉默。

毛毛蟲先開口說話。

牠問道：「你想變多大？」

「噢，多大多小都沒關係，只要不會一直變來變去就好了。」愛麗絲趕緊回答。

「我不知道囉。」毛毛蟲說。

愛麗絲什麼也沒說，她這輩子還沒被這樣反駁過，她覺得自己快發火了。

毛毛蟲問：「那你滿意現在的大小嗎？」

愛麗絲說：「先生，如果你不介意，我想再變大一點。只有三吋高，實在是太可憐了。」

毛毛蟲生氣地說道：「三吋高有什麼不好？」牠說話時還故意挺直身體。（牠正好三吋高。）

「但是我不習慣！」可憐的愛麗絲用哀求的聲音說。她心想：「希望這隻動物不要那麼容易生氣才好！」

「你遲早會習慣的。」毛毛蟲說，然後就拿起水煙袋又抽了起來。

這一次，愛麗絲耐心地等毛毛蟲自己先開口說話。幾分鐘後，毛毛蟲放下水煙袋，伸了幾個懶腰，扭扭身體，之後從蘑菇上跳了下來，爬進草叢裡，邊走邊說：「這一邊可以讓你長高，那一邊可以讓你變矮。」

「哪裡的這邊？又哪裡的那邊？」愛麗絲心裡想。

「蘑菇的這邊和那邊。」毛毛蟲說，一副好像聽到了愛麗絲在大聲發問似的。不一會兒，毛毛蟲就消失不見。

愛麗絲盯著蘑菇一會兒，想搞清楚毛毛蟲所說的那邊和這邊究竟是哪一邊。因為蘑菇整朵是圓的，根本很難分清楚。最後，愛麗絲只好伸出雙手，在蘑菇的兩側，各摘了一小片。

她對自己說：「究竟哪邊是哪邊？」她一邊拿起右手的蘑菇，輕輕地咬了一小口，想試試效果。才剛吃完，她就感到下巴一陣劇痛，原來是下巴撞到了腳。

她對於突如其來的改變感到非常害怕，但時間不允許她多想，因為她正在迅速地縮小，於是她立刻拿起另一片蘑菇想要吃一口，但她的下巴緊緊地壓在腳上，嘴巴無法張開。不過，她最後還是辦到了，費力地吞了一小口左手的蘑菇。

「我的頭終於自由了。」愛麗絲高興地說，但沒多久，她又緊張起來，因為她的肩膀不見了。當她往下看的時候，只看到長長的脖子，像莖一樣從底下遙遠的綠葉叢海中伸出來。

愛麗絲說：「那些綠綠的東西是什麼？我的肩膀又到哪裡去了？喔，可憐的手，我怎麼看不到你們？」她邊說邊揮動著雙手，但是遠處的樹葉除了一陣搖晃外，就再也沒有反應了。

M.W.T.

既然手舉起來看不到，愛麗絲只好將頭彎向手那邊，結果她很高興地發現自己的脖子可以像蛇一樣，任意地彎來彎去。她成功地將脖子優雅地彎成鋸齒狀，正準備將頭伸進底下的樹叢時，這才發現這些樹叢原來就是她剛剛漫步的樹林的上方。這時，一陣尖銳的嘶嘶聲嚇得她趕緊把頭縮回來，原來是一隻鴿子迎面衝向她的臉，還大力地振動翅膀。

「蛇！」鴿子尖叫道。

「我不是蛇，走開！」愛麗絲憤怒地說。

「蛇，我就要說你是蛇！」鴿子重複說道，但語氣稍微緩和了一些，接著又哽咽地加了一句：「我試過各種方法，但是都沒有用。」

「你在說什麼？我聽不懂。」愛麗絲說。

「我試過樹根、土堤和灌木叢。」鴿子繼續說，並沒有留意愛麗絲在說什麼。「但那些可惡的蛇，就是不肯罷手！」

愛麗絲越聽越困惑，但她想除非鴿子把話說完，不然她再多說什麼也沒有用。

鴿子說：「牠們是覺得我孵蛋還不夠辛苦嗎？我還得不分晝夜地隨時留意那些蛇，哎呀，我已經整整三個星期沒闔眼睡覺了。」

「你被騷擾，讓人很同情。」愛麗絲慢慢開始聽懂鴿子的話。

鴿子繼續說著，聲音越來越尖銳：「我好不容易找到樹林裡最高的一棵樹，以為終於可以高枕無憂了，沒想到蛇卻蠕動著身體從天而降。哼，可惡的蛇！」

「可是我說過了，我不是蛇！我是——我是——」愛麗絲說。

鴿子說：「好吧，那你是誰？我知道你想編故事來騙我！」

「我——我是一個小女孩。」愛麗絲用遲疑的語氣說，她想起今天這一天所經歷的各種變化。

鴿子很不屑地說：「說得跟真的一樣，我這一生中看過很多小女孩，就沒見過脖子長得像你這樣的小女孩。少來了，你根本就是蛇，你再怎麼否認都沒用。我猜，接下來你會跟我說，你沒有吃過蛋！」

愛麗絲很誠實地說：「我當然吃過蛋，小女孩有時也會像蛇一樣吃蛋的。」

「我才不信，如果小女孩也吃蛋的話，那麼她們也是蛇的一種，你不用再解釋了。」鴿子說。

這種說法對愛麗絲來說很新奇，讓她愣了一會兒。鴿子於是趁機加了幾句：「你現在一定是在找蛋，我太了解你們了，不管你是小女孩還是蛇，對我來說都一樣。」

「對我來說就不一樣了，我才不是來偷蛋的，就算是，我也不會想偷你的蛋，我才不喜歡吃生蛋。」愛麗絲趕緊說。

「夠了，快滾吧！」鴿子生氣地說，一邊飛回自己的巢。愛麗絲努力地想要在樹叢裡蹲下來，但脖子卻不斷地和樹枝糾纏在一起，於是她只好不時停下來將樹枝撥開。過了一會兒，她記起她的手上還有兩片蘑菇，於是她小心翼翼地吃了起來。她先咬了一小口左手的蘑菇，接著又咬了右手的那片。因此，她的身體一下子長高，一會兒又縮小，直到身體恢復正常的高度為止。

自從她的身體開始反覆地變來變去之後，已經很久沒這麼正常過了。剛開始時她還不太習慣，過了幾分鐘後，才算適應。她開始像之前一樣自言自語地說：「好啦，我的計畫已經完成一半了！剛才的變化真是令人困惑，下一分鐘會變成什麼樣子，我都不知道。不過無論如何，我總算恢復原來正常的大小了。接下來就是去找那座美麗的花園了，但該怎麼做才好呢？」愛麗絲說這話時，突然看到一塊空地，那裡有一幢約莫四呎高的房子，愛麗絲心想：「不管是誰住在裡面，以我現在這個樣子，不嚇壞他們才怪。」所以，她又咬了一口右手的蘑菇，等到身體變成九吋高，才敢向屋子走去。

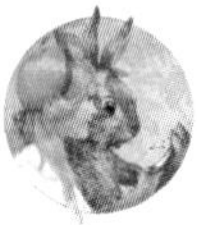

第六章

豬與胡椒粉

愛麗絲站著看了那幢房子一會兒，不知道接下來該怎麼做。突然，有一個穿制服的僕役從樹林裡跑出來（因為牠穿制服，所以愛麗絲才會認為牠是僕役，不然只從牠的臉來判斷，愛麗絲會認為牠是一條魚），用關節用力地敲著門。另一個也穿著制服、圓臉大眼睛，

長得像青蛙的僕役出來應門。愛麗絲注意到，牠們兩個都有一頭噴粉鬈髮。她很好奇牠們在做什麼，便溜出樹林，想聽牠們在說些什麼。

那個魚臉僕役從腋下拿出一封差不多和牠身體一樣大的信，交給青蛙臉僕役，用很鄭重的語氣

說：「這是給公爵夫人的，皇后邀請公爵夫人參加槌球賽。」青蛙臉僕役又以同樣認真的語氣重複了一次，只是順序調換了一下：「這封信是皇后給的，公爵夫人被邀請參加槌球賽。」

然後兩個互相鞠躬，結果頭髮竟糾纏在一起。

愛麗絲看到這一幕，忍俊不禁。她躲進樹林裡，怕自己的笑聲被聽到，等到她再探頭出來時，魚臉僕役已經不見了。只見青蛙臉僕役坐在門口的地上，楞楞地瞪著天空。

愛麗絲膽怯地走上前去敲門。

青蛙臉僕役說：「這樣敲門是沒有用的，有兩個理由，第一，我們都在門的同一邊；第二，裡面的噪音這麼大，沒有人聽得到你的敲門聲的。」的確，愛麗絲能聽到裡面不停傳出奇奇怪怪的嘈雜聲——哭叫聲、打噴嚏聲，有時還夾雜著鍋碗瓢盆摔成碎片的聲音。

愛麗絲說：「那麼請問一下，我要怎麼進去？」

「敲門或許有點用吧。」僕役不理會愛麗絲，繼續說：「假如我們兩個之間有門的話，譬如，你在門內敲門，我就會幫你開門，讓你出來。」牠說話時，還是楞楞地望著天空，愛麗絲覺得牠這樣很沒有禮貌。愛麗絲

自言自語說：「但或許牠是不得已的，牠的眼睛幾乎要長到頭頂上去了。但不管怎樣，牠總該回答我的問題——我到底要怎麼進去？」她大聲地重複問了一次。

青蛙臉僕役說：「我可能在這裡一直坐到明天吧——」

就在這時，房門突然打開，裡面丟出一個很大的盤子，朝青蛙臉僕役的臉飛去，剛好擦過了牠的鼻子，砸在牠身後的樹上，摔成了碎片。

「或許要坐到後天也說不定。」僕役還是用平淡的語氣繼續說著，好像什麼事都沒發生過似的。

愛麗絲又大聲地問了一次：「我到底要怎樣才能進去？」

「你真的想進去嗎？這是你首先要考慮的問題。」僕役說。

這個問題的確值得思考，但愛麗絲不喜歡這樣被提

醒。愛麗絲喃喃道：「真可怕，這傢伙真能辯，我快被搞瘋啦！」

僕役又藉機用不同的說法重複著牠的話：「我應該會在這裡一天天地坐下去吧。」

「那我該怎麼辦？」愛麗絲說。

「隨你高興。」僕役說罷，便吹起口哨來。

「噢，跟牠講話根本沒有用，牠是個蠢蛋！」愛麗絲用放棄的口吻說，然後打開門走進房子裡。

這扇門直接通到一個大廚房，裡面都是油煙。公爵夫人抱著一個嬰兒，坐在中間一張三腳的凳子上，而廚子站在火爐旁，正彎著身子，攪動像是裝滿湯的一大鍋東西。

「這鍋湯的胡椒一定放太多了！」愛麗絲邊打噴嚏邊說。

整個房間到處都飄著胡椒粉，就連公爵夫人也偶爾打起噴嚏，至於嬰兒，則是一會兒打噴嚏，一會兒哭，沒有間斷。在這個廚房唯一沒有打噴嚏的，就只有廚子和趴在火爐邊咧嘴大笑的大貓。

愛麗絲有些膽怯地問，不知道先開口說話會不會顯得失禮：「不好意思，可不可以請問一下，為什麼您的貓笑成那樣？」

「牠是一隻柴郡貓啊。」公爵夫人說：「懂吧。你這隻豬！」

公爵夫人說到最後一個字時，口氣突然變得很凶，愛麗絲嚇了一跳。一會兒後，愛麗絲才知道，原來公爵夫人是在罵嬰兒，不是罵愛麗絲。所以她壯起膽，繼續說：

「我不知道柴郡貓會一直裂嘴笑，事實上，我根本不知道貓竟然會笑。」

公爵夫人說：「牠們都會笑，大部分的柴郡貓都會裂嘴笑。」

「我不知道貓會笑。」愛麗絲禮貌地說，覺得能和別人對話，真是太開心了。

「你也太孤陋寡聞了，這是事實。」公爵夫人說。

愛麗絲不喜歡她講這話的口氣，便想換話題，就在她在想話題時，廚子正將一大鍋湯從火爐移開。然後立

Arthur Rackham

刻開始將手邊拿到的東西，向公爵夫人和嬰兒丟去——先是火鉗，接著是如雨一般飛來的鍋碗瓢盆。然而，即使丟來的東西砸到公爵夫人，公爵夫人也若無其事。而嬰兒本來就在哭，所以也搞不清楚是不是有被砸到。

「喂，你知不知道你在幹嘛？」愛麗絲大叫，一邊生氣地上下跳來跳去。「喂，小心他寶貝的鼻子。」一個大鍋子朝嬰兒飛去，差點把他砸死。

公爵夫人以沙啞的聲音低吼道：「如果每個人都能少管閒事，世界就會運轉得快一些。」

愛麗絲好不容易逮到可以炫耀點知識的機會，便高興地說：「那可不一定，如果運轉得更快，那晝夜就會亂掉，地球自轉（axis）一圈要二十四小時——」

公爵夫人說：「講到斧頭（axe），把她的頭給我砍下來。」

愛麗絲緊張地看著廚子，很怕她真的來砍自己的頭。還好廚子忙著攪動湯，好像沒有聽到公爵夫人說的話。她壯起膽繼續說：「是二十四小時，還是十二小時？我——」

「噢，別說了，我對數字一向很感冒！」公爵夫人說完，便又開始逗弄嬰兒，唱著催眠曲，每唱一句，就用力地搖晃嬰兒一下。

「對你的小男孩說話要嚴厲，
他打噴嚏時，要打他。
他明知道我們不喜歡，
還故意這麼做。」

合唱
（廚師和嬰兒也跟著唱和）——
「哇！哇！哇！」

公爵夫人唱到第二段時，還用力地將嬰兒搖上搖下，可憐的小東西又嚎啕大哭起來，所以愛麗絲幾乎聽不到她在唱什麼：

「我嚴厲地對我的小男孩說，
他敢打噴嚏，我就打他。
只要他喜歡，
可以盡情用胡椒！」

合唱
「哇！哇！哇！」

公爵夫人一邊將嬰兒拋給愛德絲，一邊說道：「接著！你來照顧他一下，如果你想的話！我得準備一下，

好陪皇后打槌球。」接著就匆忙地跑出去，當她離開時，廚子還向她丟了一個油鍋，不過沒有打中。

嬰兒的姿勢很奇怪，手腳張得很開，愛麗絲好不容易才接住他。「真像海星。」愛麗絲想。才抱到手上，這可憐的小東西竟像蒸氣引擎一樣呼出聲音，而且一下子彎起腰來，一會兒又伸直身子，搞得愛麗絲一開始不知道要怎麼抱他才好。

等她知道怎麼把他哄住時（她將他的身體像繩子打結一樣扭起來，然後抓緊他的右耳和左腳，以防止鬆開），便抱著嬰兒來到屋外。愛麗絲心想：「我要是不把他帶走，他不出一、兩天就會被弄死了。我如果丟下他不管，這樣算不算謀殺？」她大聲地把後面的問題講出來，而嬰兒也用咕嚕咕嚕的聲音來回應（這時他已經停止打噴嚏）。「不要發出這種咕嚕咕嚕的聲音，這不是你該有的正確表達方式。」愛麗絲說。

但嬰兒又發出了咕嚕咕嚕的聲音，愛麗絲以為他有什麼毛病，焦急地看著他的臉，結果發現他的鼻子很翹，和一般人不太一樣，像極了豬的鼻子。而他的眼睛，對嬰兒來說，也實在小得離譜。總之，愛麗絲就是不喜歡他的長相。「不過，這大概只是因為在哭的關係

吧。」她猜想，然後仔細地觀察了他的眼睛，想看裡面是不是有眼淚。

結果愛麗絲發現他一滴眼淚也沒有，她認真地說：「親愛的，你小心點！如果你變成了一隻豬，我就不理你了。」這可憐的小東西又開始哭了起來。（或者是說像豬一樣咕嚕咕嚕地叫了起來，這到底是在哭還是在叫，讓人分不清。）然後他們又靜靜地往前走了一段。

愛麗絲才心想：「我要是把他帶回家，要怎麼處理呢？」這時，嬰兒又大叫了起來，愛麗絲緊張地看著他的臉，這次錯不了了，他的的確確就是一隻豬。愛麗絲覺得要再繼續抱著他實在是太荒謬了。

於是，她將這個小東西放下來，看著牠靜靜晃進樹林裡，才鬆了一口氣。她自言自語說：「牠長大後一定是個醜巴巴的小孩，不過，就一隻豬來說，還算是滿帥的。」於是她開始回想她所認識的小孩，有沒有長得像豬一樣醜的。她對自己說：「如果有人知道要怎麼改變他們的長相就好了——」這時，她突然看到那隻咧嘴笑的貓就坐在前方幾碼遠的樹枝上，讓她吃了小小一驚。

貓看到愛麗絲時，照樣咧著嘴笑。貓看起來沒有惡意，但她心想：牠的爪子那麼長，牙齒那利，我還是客氣一點比較好。

「柴郡貓。」愛麗絲小心翼翼地說，不知道牠喜不喜歡這個稱呼，只見貓把嘴再咧開了些，愛麗絲想：「到目前為止，牠還很高興。」於是她繼續說：「請問我該走哪條路呢？」

「那要看你想去哪裡。」貓說。

「哪兒都行。」愛麗絲說。

貓說：「那你就怎麼走都行。」

「——只要能離開這裡。」愛麗絲解釋說。

貓說：「噢，沒問題，你走遠些就行了。」

愛麗覺得這個回答倒是也沒錯，於是改問道：「住在這附近的都是什麼樣的人？」

貓揮舞著右爪說：「那個方向，住著一個帽商，另一個方向，」又揮著左爪說：「住著一隻三月兔。要找誰隨便你，不過，他們都是瘋子。」

「我不想跟瘋子在一起。」愛麗絲說。

貓說：「噢，那可能沒辦法，因為這裡的人都是瘋子，我是瘋子，你也是瘋子。」

「你怎麼知道我是瘋子？」愛麗絲問。

「瘋子才會來這裡。」貓說。

愛麗絲覺得這種說法根本不成立，於是又問：「那你又如何知道你是瘋子？」

貓說：「這麼說好了，狗不是瘋子，對吧？」

「我想對吧。」愛麗絲說。

貓繼續說：「你一定看過狗生氣時會咆哮、高興時會搖尾巴吧，但我呢，我高興時會咆哮，生氣時會搖尾巴，所以，我是瘋子。」

「我們說那是貓的嗚嗚聲，不是咆哮聲。」愛麗絲說。

「隨便你怎麼說。」貓說：「你今天要跟皇后打槌球嗎？」

「我很想去，但我沒有接到邀請函。」愛麗絲說。

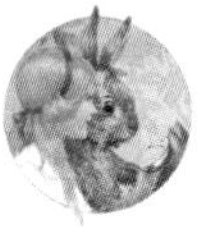

「那麼我們就在那裡見啦。」說完，貓就消失了。

這並沒有讓愛麗絲吃驚，稀奇古怪的事情她已經見怪不怪了。她看著貓剛才坐的地方時，又突然現身。

「我差點忘了問你，那個嬰兒怎麼樣了？」貓說。

「牠變成一隻豬了。」愛麗絲不假思索地回答，好像貓的出現是一件很自然的事。

「果然不出我所料。」話說完，貓又消失無蹤了。

愛麗絲等了一會兒，以為貓會再出現，但並沒有。過了一會兒，愛麗絲便朝貓所指的三月兔所住的方向走去。她自言自語說：「我之前見過帽商，三月兔應該會比較有趣吧。不過現在是五月了，三月兔大概不會那麼瘋吧——至少不會像三月發情時那麼瘋。」說著說著，不經意抬頭一望，看到貓這時坐在另一棵樹的樹枝上。

「你剛剛說的是豬（pig）還是無花果（fig）？」貓問。

愛麗絲回答道：「我說的是豬，我希望你不要一直這樣突然出現、又突然消失，會讓人頭昏眼花。」

貓回答說：「好吧！」這次，牠緩慢地消失，先從尾巴末端，然後到身體消失不見，最後只剩笑臉懸在半空中。

愛麗絲心想：「沒有笑臉的貓，我看過很多，可是有笑臉卻沒有貓，我還是第一次看到，這真是我這輩子見過最奇怪的事了。」

她走沒多遠，就看到三月兔的房子，她猜想那應該就是兔子的家吧，因為煙囪的形狀很像兔子的耳朵，而且屋頂還覆蓋了兔毛。那是一幢大房子，愛麗絲不敢馬上走上前去。她先吃了幾口左手上的蘑菇，讓自己變成兩呎高後，才膽怯地走過去。她對自己說：「我還是假設裡面住著一隻瘋兔子比較保險，真是的，說不定去帽商那裡會比較好！」

10/6

第七章

瘋狂茶會

房子前一棵的樹下擺了一張長桌子，帽商和三月兔正在喝茶，一隻睡鼠就坐在他們中間睡覺，而帽商和三月兔就把睡鼠當墊子，把手肘靠在牠身上講話。愛麗絲心想：「睡鼠一定很不舒服，不過牠已經睡著了，應該不會介意吧。」

這張桌子很大，三個人卻都擠在一角。當牠們看到愛麗絲來時，連忙叫道：「沒空位了！沒空位了！」愛麗絲生氣地說：「空位還這麼多！」於是她在桌子的一端，拉了一張有靠背和扶手的大椅子，坐了下來。

「來點葡萄酒吧。」三月兔用慫恿的語氣說。

愛麗絲看了看桌上的東西，發現桌上除了茶以外，什麼也沒有，便說：「這裡沒有葡萄酒。」

「對啊，我們這裡沒有葡萄酒。」三月兔說。

愛麗絲生氣地說：「那你還請我喝葡萄酒，這是很不禮貌的。」

「你也沒經過我的同意就坐下來，一樣很不禮貌。」三月兔說。

愛麗絲說：「我又不知道這是你的桌子，何況桌子那麼大，不只可以坐三個人。」

「你的頭髮該剪了。」帽商說。他很好奇地觀察了愛麗絲一陣子，這是他所說的第一句話。

愛麗絲有點嚴厲地說：「你應該學習不要做人身攻擊，這樣很無禮。」

聽到愛麗絲這麼說，帽商的眼睛瞪得大大的，他說：「為什麼烏鴉會長得像寫字桌？」

愛麗絲心想：「現在我們應該輕鬆一下，真高興，他們在出謎語了——」於是，她大聲說道：「我想我猜得到。」

「你是說，你覺得你能猜到答案？」三月兔問。

「沒錯。」愛麗絲說。

「那麼就應該『說出你想的』（say what you mean）。」三月兔繼續說。

愛麗絲趕緊回答道：「當然，至少『我想的就是我說的』（I mean what I say）——這是一樣的。」

帽商說：「才怪，不一樣！你怎麼不說『我看到我吃的東西』和『我吃我看到的東西』是一樣的意思？」

三月兔又加了一句：「你乾脆說『我喜歡我得到的東西』和『我得到我喜歡的東西』是一樣的意思。」

這時，睡鼠半夢半醒地附和了一句：「你乾脆說『我睡覺時在呼吸』和『我呼吸時在睡覺』是一樣的意思！」

帽商說：「這個對你來說是一樣的。」話說到這裡，大家突然停了下來，茶會一片安靜。愛麗絲努力回想烏鴉和書桌的謎語，卻怎麼也想不出來。

帽商首先打破沉默。他轉向愛麗絲問道：「今天是幾號？」他從口袋拿出手錶，緊張地看著，還不時搖晃，然後拿到耳邊來聽。

愛麗絲想了一會兒，回答說：「今天是四號。」

「晚了兩天！」帽商嘆了一口氣，然後生氣地看著三月兔繼續說：「我早就告訴你，用奶油是行不通的！」

「那已經是最好的奶油了。」三月兔低聲地回答。

帽商咕噥道：「對了，一定是有麵包屑掉進去才會這樣，你不應該用切麵包的刀子來弄。」

三月兔拿起了那只錶，憂心地看看錶，然後把錶浸泡在茶杯裡，再看了一次。不過，牠實在想不出有什麼話比剛才說的更好，只好重複剛剛說的話：「那已經是最好的奶油了。」

愛麗絲有點兒好奇地看了看那只錶，說：「這只錶真奇怪，只顯示日期，卻沒有時間。」

帽商喃喃道：「為什麼要有時間，你的錶有顯示年份嗎？」

愛麗絲不假思索地回答說：「當然沒有囉，可是那是因為年份能維持一段很長的時間不會變。」

「我的時間也是這樣啊。」帽商說。

愛麗絲感到困惑，因為她完全不了解帽商的意思，可是他和她的確是講英文啊。「我不太懂你的意思。」愛麗絲很有禮貌地問。

「睡鼠又睡著了。」帽商說。他拿了一壺熱茶，倒一些在睡鼠的鼻子上。

睡鼠沒睜開眼睛，不耐煩地搖搖頭說：「當然，當然，我也打算這麼說。」

「你猜出答案了嗎？」帽商對愛麗絲說。

愛麗絲回答：「沒有，我放棄，答案是什麼？」

「我不知道。」帽商說。

「我也不知道。」三月兔說。

愛麗絲不耐煩地嘆了一口氣說：「我覺得你們應該把時間花在更有意義的事情上，問一些沒有答案的謎語，是在浪費時間。」

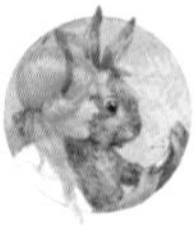

帽商說：「如果你和我一樣了解時間，就不會說在浪費『它』了，而是浪費『他』。」

「我不懂你的意思。」愛麗絲說。

「你當然不懂。」帽商輕蔑地搖搖頭說：「我敢說你從來沒跟時間說過話！」

愛麗絲小心地回答：「可能沒有吧，但是我在學音樂的時候，我得按時間來打拍子。」

帽商說：「喔，這就難怪了，他可禁不住打。如果你和他好好相處，他就會照你的意思來改變時鐘上的時間。舉例來說，假設現在是早上九點，也就是要上課的時間，你只要對時間暗示一聲，不一會兒工夫，就會到下午一點半，也就是吃飯的時間了。」

（「如果真是這樣就好了。」三月兔輕聲對自己說。）

愛麗絲思考了一下說：「如果你說的是真的，那當然很好，不過，如果那時我還不餓，怎麼辦？」

「剛開始你可能還不會餓，但你可以把時間停在一點半，直到你高興為止。」帽商說。

愛麗絲問：「你就是這麼做的嗎？」

帽商難過地搖搖頭，回答說：「沒有！我們去年三

In this Style
10/6

月吵了一架——就在牠發情前（一邊將湯匙指向三月兔）——我們受邀去參加紅心皇后所舉辦的音樂盛會，我負責唱一首歌：

一閃一閃，小蝙蝠，
我很好奇你在哪裡。

你大概聽過這首歌吧？」

「我聽過類似的歌。」愛麗絲說。

帽商繼續說：「那你應該知道接下來是這麼唱的：

你飛翔在天空，
好像天空的茶盤。
一閃一閃——」

這時，睡鼠抖了一下，竟在睡夢中唱了起來：「一閃一閃，一閃一閃——」牠不停地唱著，別人只好往牠身上掐一把，好讓牠停下來。

帽商說：「那時我第一段都還沒唱完，皇后就跳起來大叫：『他在謀殺時間啊！把他的頭砍下來！』」

「好野蠻喔！」愛麗絲驚叫。

帽商繼續傷心地說：「從那次之後，他就不肯照我的要求去做了，時間也就永遠停在六點鐘了。」

愛麗絲突然想到一件事，便問道：「你桌上擺了那麼多茶具，就是因為這個關係，對不對？」

「沒錯，就是因為這樣，所以永遠是下午茶時間，害得我們沒有時間清洗茶具。」帽商嘆了一口氣說。

「所以你們就這樣不斷地換位置？」愛麗絲說。

「沒錯，東西用過了，就換新位子。」帽商說。

愛麗絲大膽地問：「那如果你們又回到最初的位置，那會怎樣？」

三月兔打了個哈欠，打斷他們的話說：「我們換個話題好嗎？我已經聽膩了，我建議這位年輕的小姐講個故事給我們聽。」

愛麗絲對這個提議感到很驚恐，說：「我沒有什麼故事好講的。」

於是他們大聲叫道：「讓睡鼠來講好了！起來

了，睡鼠！」他們立刻在睡鼠的兩側各捏了一把。

睡鼠懶洋洋地睜開眼睛，發出沙啞而微弱的聲音：「我才沒有睡著，你們講的每一個字，我都聽見了。」

「那就講個故事給我們聽吧！」三月兔說。

「對啊，講吧！」愛麗絲祈求說。

帽商又加了一句：「快點說，不然故事還沒講完，你又要睡著了。」

於是睡鼠開始以很快的速度說：「很久很久以前，有三位姊妹，叫做愛絲、蕾絲和蒂莉，她們住在井底——」

「那麼她們要靠什麼維生？」愛麗絲對吃喝的問題總是比較有興趣。

睡鼠想了一會兒說：「她們靠糖漿維生。」

「那不可能，會生病的。」愛麗絲溫和地說。

「沒錯，她們是生很嚴重的病。」睡鼠說。

愛麗絲想像著這種不尋常的生活方式，但卻越來越迷惑，所以她繼續說：「可是為什麼她們要住在井底呢？」

三月兔非常誠懇地對愛麗絲說：「多喝一點茶吧。」

「我什麼都還沒喝，所以不能『多』喝點。」愛麗絲悻悻然地說。

「你的意思是說，不能『少』喝點。不過，多喝點比什麼都不喝還容易。」帽商說。

「沒有人在問你的意見！」愛麗絲說。

「現在誰在做人身攻擊？」帽商得意地說。

愛麗絲不知道要如何回答才是，只好給自己倒些茶，吃了幾口奶油麵包，之後轉向睡鼠，重複剛才的問題：「為什麼她們要住在井底？」

睡鼠想了一會兒，說：「因為那是個糖漿的井。」

「天底下才沒有這種東西！」愛麗絲開始變得很生氣，帽商和三月兔對她發出噓聲，睡鼠也生氣地說：「如果你再這樣沒禮貌，你就自己來把故事說完。」

愛麗絲虛心地說：「對不起，請繼續說！我不會再打斷你了。我敢說，這世上一定有這樣的井。」

「的確有一個！」睡鼠生氣地說著，但牠答應繼續說故事：「這三個姊妹便開始學習汲取。」

「她們要汲取什麼？」愛麗絲說，她轉眼就忘記剛才說過不再插話的。

這次睡鼠立刻就說：「糖漿啊。」

帽商插嘴說：「我要一個乾淨的茶杯，我們換個位置吧。」

他邊說邊換了個位子，睡鼠坐了帽商原先的位子，三月兔坐在睡鼠原來的座位，愛麗絲於是很不情願地換到三月兔的位子。換過位置之後，只有帽商占了便宜，愛麗絲則很慘，因為三月兔把牛奶罐打翻到盤子裡。

愛麗絲不想再惹睡鼠生氣，便小心翼翼地問：「但我不懂，她們從哪裡汲取糖漿啊？」

帽商說：「你可以從水井汲出水，當然也可以從糖漿井裡汲出糖漿囉！笨蛋！」

愛麗絲不理會帽商的話，對睡鼠說：「但是她們就待在井裡耶。」

「她們當然是待在井裡啊。」睡鼠說。

睡鼠的回答讓可憐的愛麗絲更加困惑，她索性讓睡鼠繼續講一會兒，不再打斷牠的話。

「她們開始學習如何汲取，」睡鼠繼續說，因為牠太睏了，所以打了個哈欠，揉揉眼睛，「她們汲取各式各樣的東西——所有英文字母M開頭的東西——」

「為什麼是M開頭的東西？」

「為什麼不是？」三月兔說。

愛麗絲不發一語。

這時睡鼠已經閉上眼睛，眼看就要睡著了，但帽商趕緊掐牠一下，牠便醒了過來，抖抖身子，繼續說：「她們開始汲取M開頭的東西，像是捕鼠器（mouse-traps）、月亮（moon）、回憶（memory）和許多（muchness），就是你說事情『大同小異』（much of a muchness）的那個『許多』（muchness）。你有看過汲取『許多』這種事嗎？」

愛麗絲很困惑地說：「既然你這麼問，我只能說，沒有——」

「既然沒有，你就別說話！」帽商說。

愛麗絲再也無法忍受這種粗魯的態度，她很嫌惡地站起身，轉頭就走。這時，睡鼠立刻又睡著了，而三月兔和帽商一點也沒注意到愛麗絲的離去，雖然她回頭看了一、兩次，希望牠們能叫她回來。但當她最後一次回頭時，卻看到他們在把睡鼠塞進茶壺裡。

愛麗絲在樹林裡選了一條路，邊走邊說：「不管怎樣，我是不會再回到那裡了！這是我這輩子參加過最愚蠢的茶會！」

話才剛說完，她就看到樹上有一道門，她心想：「好奇怪喔，不過，我今天遇到的事情，有哪件事不是很奇怪的呢？我想我最好立刻走進去看看。」於是，她便走了進去。

進去之後，愛麗絲發現自己又來到了那個長廳，小玻璃桌就在她身旁，她對自己說：「這次一定沒問題的。」然後她就拿起金色的小鑰匙，打開通往花園的小門，接著她拿出蘑菇吃了幾口（她留了一小塊在自己的口袋裡），把身體縮小到一呎高，以便走進那條小通道。最後，她終於來到了那座美麗的花園，置身在奼紫嫣紅的花圃和清涼的噴泉之中。

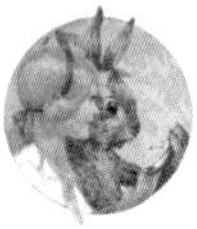

第八章

皇后的槌球大賽

花園入口處種了一棵大玫瑰樹，樹上開著白色的玫瑰，樹旁圍了三個園丁[†]，正忙著把玫瑰塗成紅色。愛麗絲覺得很奇怪，便走上前去，看他們在做什麼。當她剛靠近時，聽到他們其中有一個人說：「小心哪，五點！不要把油漆潑到我身上！」

五點生氣地說：「沒辦法，七點撞到了我的手肘了。」

七點抬頭說：「對啦，五點，反正都是別人的錯。」

「你最好不要再囉唆了，昨天我才聽到皇后說要砍你的頭！」五點說。

「為什麼？」剛剛第一個講話的園丁問道。

「不關你的事，兩點！」七點說。

「怎麼不關他的事，他本來應該拿洋蔥給廚師的，結果不小心拿成鬱金香球根了。」五點說。

† 園丁都是黑桃 spade，而spade 有整理花園的意思

七點聽到，馬上丟下刷子，開始說：「這樣說太不公平了——」突然他瞧到愛麗絲站在那裡看著他們，於是立刻把溜到嘴邊的話吞回去，其他兩個人四處張望了一下，然後三個人一起彎腰向愛麗絲鞠躬。

愛麗絲有些膽怯地問：「你們可不可以告訴我，為什麼要把玫瑰花塗上油漆？」

五點和七點什麼話也沒說，只是看著兩點，兩點於是低聲地回答：「小姐，事情是這樣的，本來這裡應該種一棵紅玫瑰樹，結果我們不小心種成了白玫瑰樹。如果皇后發現了這件事，我們的腦袋就不保了。所以我們得趁皇后還沒到這裡來之前，盡我們所能——」就在這時，原本緊張地四下張望花園的五點，突然大叫：「皇后來了！皇后來了！」於是三個園丁立刻將臉朝下地趴在地上。遠處傳來紛沓的腳步聲，愛麗絲四周觀望，想看看皇后長什麼樣子。

首先映入眼簾的是十名拿著棍棒†的士兵，這些士兵都長得和三位園丁一模一樣，扁扁的長方形身材，手腳就長在長方形的四個角落。接下來是十位宮廷的大臣†，身上裝飾著許多紅磚，和士兵一樣倆倆並排行

† 棍棒是 club，所以士兵就是梅花（club）的圖案
† 大臣是方塊（Diamond）的圖案

走。再來是十個皇室的小孩，一對對蹦蹦跳跳愉快地手牽手走過來，每個孩子身上都裝飾著許多紅心†。再接下來的是客人，那些客人大都是國王和皇后。在這群人當中，愛麗絲認出了白兔子，牠看起來緊張兮兮的樣子，嘴裡唸唸有詞，對著唸到的東西作出笑臉。當牠經過愛麗絲時，並沒有注意到她。然後是紅心侍者，手裡捧著深紅色的天鵝絨墊，上面放著國王的皇冠。走在這個壯觀隊伍的最後面，是紅心國王和皇后。

愛麗絲不知道自己是否要像三個園丁一樣，臉朝下地趴在地上，因為她不記得聽過有這種規矩，她心想：「如果臉朝下地趴在地上，不就什麼都看不到了嗎？」所以，她還是站著，等他們走過面前。

當整個隊伍行經至愛麗絲面前時，大家都停下來盯著她瞧。皇后聲色俱厲地問紅心侍者：「這是誰？」侍者鞠了個躬，笑而未答。

皇后不耐煩地搖搖頭，罵道：「白痴！」然後轉向愛麗絲繼續問道：「孩子，你叫什麼名字？」

「我叫愛麗絲，親愛的皇后陛下。」愛麗絲非常禮貌地回答，但是又對自己加了一句：「他們只是一堆撲克牌罷了，我幹嘛怕他們？」

† 皇室是紅心（Heart）的圖案

「這幾個又是誰？」皇后指著趴在玫瑰樹周圍的三名園丁問，由於他們都是臉朝地地趴著，從背後看起來的花色都是一樣，所以分辨不出來誰是園丁、誰是士兵、誰是臣子，還是說這是她自己的三個小孩。

「我怎麼會知道，這不關我的事。」愛麗絲說，被自己突如其來的勇氣嚇了一跳。

皇后氣得滿臉通紅，像頭野獸地瞪了一下愛麗絲，尖叫道：「砍了她的頭！砍了——」

「少廢話！」愛麗絲毫不退怯地大聲說道，皇后立刻閉上了嘴。

國王將手放在皇后的臂膀，溫和地說：「親愛的，她只是個小孩子，別和她一般見識！」

皇后氣得掉頭不理他，然後對侍者說：「把他們翻過來！」

侍者遵照皇后的指示，小心翼翼用腳把他們翻過來。

「站起來！」皇后尖聲大叫。三名園丁立刻跳起來，向國王、皇后、皇子們和在場的所有人一一鞠躬。

皇后尖聲吼道：「不要再鞠躬了！你們搞得我頭昏眼花。」然後，她將頭轉向玫瑰樹，問道：「你們剛才在這裡做什麼？」

「皇后陛下，」兩點將一邊的膝蓋跪了下來，謙卑地說：「我們正努力——」

皇后一邊端詳玫瑰，一邊說：「我明白了！把他們的頭給砍下來！」整個隊伍又繼續地往前走，留下三名士兵負責處決三名不幸的園丁。三名園丁立刻跑向愛麗絲尋求保護。

「你們不應該被砍頭的！」愛麗絲說，於是將三名園丁藏在附近的一個大花盆裡。三名士兵找了園丁一會兒，找不到後，便快速大步追上前面的隊伍。

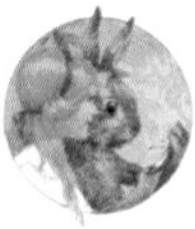

「他們的頭砍下了沒？」皇后咆哮道。

「皇后陛下！他們的頭已經不見了。」士兵們大聲地回答。

「那就好！」皇后大聲說：「你會玩槌球嗎？」

士兵們沒回答，只是把眼光投向愛麗絲，顯然這個問題是針對她而來的。

「會啊！」愛麗絲大聲地回答。

「那就一起走吧！」皇后大聲說，於是愛麗絲就加入了他們的隊伍，猜測著等一下會發生什麼事。

這時，愛麗絲身旁有一個怯生生的聲音說：「今天——今天天氣不錯喔！」白兔子跟在她旁邊走著，緊張兮兮地窺視她的臉。

「非常好，咦，公爵夫人呢？」愛麗絲回答。

「噓！噓！」白兔低聲快速地說，還緊張地環顧周圍，然後踮起腳尖，把嘴巴湊到愛麗絲的耳邊說：「她被判死刑了。」

「為什麼？」愛麗絲問。

「你是說『真可惜』嗎？」兔子問道。

「不是，我並不是覺得可惜，我是說『為什麼』。」愛麗絲說。

「她打了皇后一個耳光——」兔子說。愛麗絲笑了出來，白兔害怕地耳語說：「噓！小聲點。這樣皇后會聽到。公爵夫人遲到太久，所以皇后就說——」

「各就各位！」皇后發出雷吼般的聲音說道。大家開始互相推擠，往各個方向分散。不過一會兒後，大家都各就各位，比賽便開始了。愛麗絲這輩子沒看過這麼奇怪的槌球比賽，球場到處是隆起的山脊和犁溝，槌球是活生生的刺蝟，球槌是活生生的紅鶴，士兵趴在地上弓起著身子，當作球門。

首先，對愛麗絲來說，最大的困難是要如何操縱紅鶴。她成功地先將牠的身體藏在腋下，弄了個舒適的姿勢後，讓紅鶴的兩隻腳懸空在外面，然後把牠的脖子弄直，準備用紅鶴的頭去打刺蝟。這時，紅鶴轉過頭來，用疑惑的神情看著愛麗絲，愛麗絲忍不住笑了出來。當她又重新把牠的頭擺好準備開始打時，原本捲成一團的刺蝟，伸出刺想要逃走，讓愛麗絲感到很生氣。還有，當她要把刺蝟丟出去時，又發現球場都是凹凹凸凸的田埂。再來就是，彎起身子的士兵會突然站起來，走到球場的另一邊去。很快地，愛麗絲得到一個結論：這場槌球比賽實在太困難了。

所有的參賽者都不輪流上場就立刻玩了起來，有時候爭吵，有時候為了爭刺蝟而打起來，皇后還會不時大發雷霆，四處跺腳，然後三不五時大吼：「把他拖出去斬了！」或是「把她拖出去斬了！」

愛麗絲感到很不安，雖然到目前為止，她還沒和皇后發生過爭執，但她知道這是遲早會發生的事。她心想：「到時候我該怎麼辦？這裡的人那麼愛砍人家的頭，我很好奇，再這樣下去，還會有多少人活著？」

於是她到處張望，想辦法要偷偷地溜走。突然，她注意到半空中浮現一個奇怪的影像，剛開始，她不解那是什麼東西，看了一會兒後，才發現那是一張笑臉。她對自己說：「不就是那隻柴郡貓嗎？終於有人可以跟我講講話了。」

當貓的嘴清楚可見時，牠問道：「球打得如何？」

愛麗絲等到貓的眼睛出現時，才向牠點點頭。她

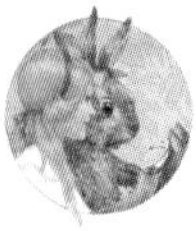

想：「牠的耳朵還沒出現，講了可能也聽不到吧，所以至少要等到一隻耳朵出現才行。」過了一會兒，等到貓的頭全部浮現，愛麗絲放下紅鶴球槌，開始和貓聊起這場球賽，她很高興終於有人聽她說話了。而貓似乎認為露出頭就夠了，其他部位就沒有現身出來。

愛麗絲抱怨說：「我覺得大家都投機取巧，又吵得很兇，吵得連自己的聲音都快聽不到了。而且比賽好像也沒有特別的規矩，就算有，也沒有人理會那些規則。你不知道用活生生的動物來當球具，有多難玩啊。譬如，我要打進球門，球門卻在球場的另一邊閒逛，而輪到我打皇后的刺蝟槌球時，刺蝟卻一看到我就逃跑。」

「你喜歡皇后嗎？」貓低聲問。

「一點也不喜歡，她那麼——」愛麗絲說，但還沒講完時，就注意到皇后在她後面偷聽，於是她便繼續說：「那麼厲害，我根本贏不了她，再玩下去也沒什麼意思。」

皇后微笑著走開了。

「你在跟誰說話啊？」國王走近問，很好奇地看著半空中的貓頭。

「容我介紹，牠是我的朋友柴郡貓。」愛麗絲說。

國王說：「我一點也不喜歡牠的表情，不過，如果牠喜歡的話，我可以讓牠親吻一下我的手。」

「我才不要。」貓說。

國王說：「不得無禮！也不准這樣看著我。」說話時，竟躲到愛麗絲的背後。

「貓可以看著國王的，我在一本書上看過這樣的規定，但我忘了是哪本書了。」愛麗絲說。

「不管怎樣，我就是要除掉牠。」國王堅決地說，這時皇后正好經過他們，國王叫住了皇后，說：「親愛的，你來幫我除掉這隻貓！」

不論大小事，皇后解決問題的方法就只有一個：「把他的頭給砍了！」而且皇后說這句話的時候，連正眼也不瞧他們一眼。

「我來親自挑選劊子手。」國王興奮地說，然後轉身去找人。

愛麗絲聽到皇后在遠處激動地大叫，便想回去看看比賽進行得如何。愛麗絲已經聽到皇后處決三個球員了，只因為他們錯過了自己的順序。愛麗絲很不喜歡這個場面，整場球賽一片混亂，所以她也不知道是不是該輪到自己了，所以她便先去找她的刺蝟槌球。

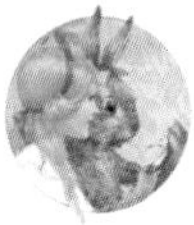

她的刺蝟槌球正在跟另一隻刺蝟槌球打架，這正是把球打出去的最佳時機，但糟糕的是，她的紅鶴球槌卻跑到了花園的另一邊，愛麗絲看到牠正徒勞地想飛到樹上去。

當她好不容易把紅鶴抓回來時，兩隻刺蝟已經打完架，跑得不見蹤影。愛麗絲心想：「沒關係，反正所有的球門士兵都跑到球場的另一邊去了。」因此，她就把紅鶴夾在腋下，不再讓牠跑掉，然後繼續和她的朋友多聊一下。

當她回到柴郡貓的旁邊時，驚訝地發現牠身旁圍著一大群人。劊子手、國王和皇后三人爭論得不可開交，其他人則神色不安地靜靜看著他們三人。

愛麗絲一出現，三個人立刻圍了過來，要她主持公道，他們立刻重複了個人的論點，但愛麗絲根本搞不懂他們在說什麼。

劊子手的看法是，沒有身體，就無法把頭從身體上砍下來。他以前沒做過這種事，這輩子也不想破例。

國王認為，劊子手在胡說八道，他認為只要有頭就能砍。

皇后就說，如果不趕快把這件事解決，她要把當

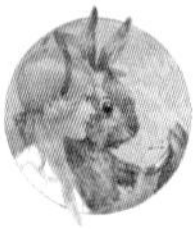

場所有的人都砍了。（就是這句話，讓所有人面色凝重。）

愛麗絲不曉得該說什麼，只好說：「這隻貓是公爵夫人養的，你們最好去問問她的意見。」

皇后對劊子手說：「她被關在牢裡，把她帶過來。」於是劊子手像箭一樣地跑開。

劊子手一離開，貓的頭便慢慢地消失了。當劊子手將公爵夫人帶來時，貓的頭就完全不見了。國王和劊子手氣急敗壞地找貓，而其他人則回到球場繼續比賽。

第九章

假烏龜的故事

「親愛的老朋友，你不知道我看到你有多高興。」公爵夫人邊說邊親熱地挽著愛麗絲的手，並肩走著。

看到她這麼親切的態度，愛麗絲也覺得很高興，她心裡想著，或許是因為第一次在廚房遇到的時候，是胡椒粉讓公爵夫人脾氣變得這麼暴躁的。

愛麗絲對自己說：「如果我是公爵夫人（雖然這種可能性不大），我才不會在廚房裡放任何的胡椒粉，就算湯裡面沒放胡椒粉，還是一樣好喝啊！可能就是胡椒粉讓人脾氣變得火爆。」她很高興自己又發現了一項新規則。「醋讓人講起話來酸溜溜的，甘菊可以讓人變得尖酸刻薄，麥芽糖之類的東西能使小孩脾氣變得乖巧溫馴，我真希望大人也知道這些規則就好了，那他們就不會這麼吝嗇，不讓小孩吃糖了——」

這時她差一點忘了公爵夫人的存在，所以當她聽到公爵夫人湊到她的耳朵講話時，不禁嚇了一跳。「親愛的，你一定是在想別的事情，不然為什麼都不說話？現

在我還不能將這些事情所隱含的道德教訓告訴你，不過等一下我就會想起來了。」

「或許根本就沒有什麼道德教訓。」愛麗絲大膽地說。

公爵夫人說：「去，去，真是孩子氣。每件事都隱含有啟示，就看你有沒有用心去發現。」說著，身子又更挨近了愛麗絲。

愛麗絲不喜歡公爵夫人靠她這麼近，第一，因為公爵夫人長得很醜，第二，公爵夫人的高度剛好可以把下巴靠在愛麗絲的肩膀上，不幸的，她的下巴又很尖，而愛麗絲不願失禮，只好盡量忍耐了。「比賽好像進行得還不錯。」她說。

公爵夫人說：「沒錯，這件事所隱含的道德教訓就是，『喔，愛，愛能讓世界轉動！』」

愛麗絲輕聲說：「但是有人說，少管閒事才能讓世界轉動！」

「哎呀，意思差不多嘛！」公爵夫人一邊說，一邊將她的尖下巴往愛麗絲的肩膀敲了幾下，然後又加了一句：「這所隱含的道德教訓，是『多思考，可以讓你言之有物。』†」

† 改編自俚語 Take care of the pence and the pounds will take care of themselves.

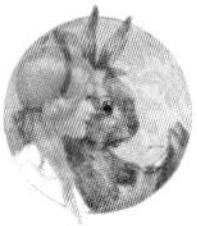

愛麗絲心裡想：「她很愛講仁義道德！」

「你一定覺得很奇怪，為什麼我怎麼不摟你的腰？」公爵夫人說，她停頓了一會兒，又繼續說：「那是因為我不清楚你手上那隻紅鶴的脾氣，我可以做個實驗嗎？」

「牠可能會咬人喔。」愛麗絲小心地回答，擔心公爵夫人會有輕率的舉動。

公爵夫人說：「沒錯，紅鶴和芥末都會咬人，這就是所謂的『物以類聚』。」

「但芥末又不是鳥類。」愛麗絲說。

公爵夫人說：「沒錯，你的頭腦還很清楚嘛！」

「我想芥末應該是礦物吧。」愛麗絲說。

「那是當然的囉！」公爵夫人說，好像愛麗絲說什麼都對。「這附近有一大片芥末礦藏，它帶給我們的啟示就是，『我擁有的越多，你擁有的就越少』。」

愛麗絲沒注意公爵夫人最後在說什麼，就大聲地叫道：「喔，我知道了，芥末是一種植物，雖然看起來不像，不過它的確是植物的一種。」

公爵夫人說：「我很同意你說的，這件事帶給我們的教訓就是，『做你自己』，簡單來說，『千萬不要被別人心目中的你所影響，即使別人心目中的你，和過去

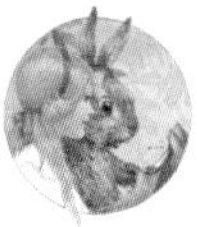

的你、現在的你有所不同，但你就是你。』」

愛麗絲禮貌地說：「如果我能把你的話寫下來，我想我會更了解意思，不然我很難跟上你說話的速度。」

「這沒什麼，我多的是道理可說呢！」公爵夫人心花怒放地說。

愛麗絲說：「那就不用勞煩你再說了。」

「怎麼會麻煩呢？我就把我剛剛說的話，當作禮物送給你好了。」公爵夫人說。

愛麗絲不敢大聲將這些話說出來，只在心裡想：「好廉價的禮物！幸好人們沒有送這種生日禮物的習慣。」

「又在想事情了？」公爵夫人問，然後又用尖下巴在她肩膀上敲了一下。

「我有權利想事情。」愛麗絲嚴厲地回了一句，因為她快要失去耐性了。

公爵夫人說：「對啊，就像豬有飛的權利，這個教訓——」

就在這時，愛麗絲發現公爵夫人的聲音越來越小，講到她最愛的「教訓」這個詞時，挽著愛麗絲的手也開始發抖起來。愛麗絲抬頭一看，原來是皇后來到她們的面前，雙手交叉，皺著眉頭，一副風雨欲來的樣子。

公爵夫人低聲微弱地說：「皇后陛下，今天天氣真不錯啊！」

「我現在慎重警告你們，你們要立刻走開，還是要立刻腦袋不保，自己做決定！」皇后邊踱著腳邊咆哮。

公爵夫人於是做出決定，立刻走掉。

皇后對愛麗絲說：「我們繼續去打球吧。」愛麗絲嚇得一句話也不敢說，只好慢慢跟隨著皇后回到球場。

來賓趁皇后不在時，紛紛跑到樹蔭下休息，但一看到皇后回來，趕緊回到球場比賽。皇后警告他們，只要比賽耽誤一秒鐘，他們就小命不保。

比賽進行中，皇后還是一如往常不斷和其他球員爭吵，大叫道：「砍下他的頭！」或「砍下她的頭！」那些被宣判死刑的人，會被士兵監禁扣留，所以原本應該擔任球門的士兵，就要放下工作起身離開。因此，比賽不到半小時，球場上就沒有球門，只剩下國王、皇后和愛麗絲三位球員，其他所有的人都被扣留，被判斬首的處決。

最後皇后只好停止比賽，喘著氣問愛麗絲說：「你看過假烏龜†嗎？」

† Mock Turtle 是一道英國料理的名稱

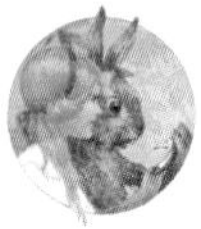

愛麗絲說：「沒看過，假烏龜是什麼我都不知道。」

「假烏龜就是用來煮假烏龜湯的嘛。」皇后說。

愛麗絲說：「我沒看過，也沒聽過什麼假烏龜。」

皇后說：「那就走吧，牠會把牠的故事告訴你的。」

當他們一起離開時，愛麗絲聽到國王低聲地對大家說：「你們全被赦免了。」愛麗絲心想：「這還差不多！」因為皇后下令處決這麼多人，她很不開心。

很快地，他們來到一隻半鷹半獅的怪獸†旁，牠正躺在陽光下睡覺。（如果你不知道什麼是半鷹半獅的怪獸，請參考圖。）皇后說：「起來了，懶骨頭！帶這位小姑娘去見假烏龜，聽牠說自己的故事。我得趕快回去，還有一些人等著我處決。」說完，皇后便走掉，留下愛麗絲和那隻怪獸。愛麗絲一點都不喜歡這隻怪獸的長相，不過，比起和脾氣暴躁的皇后一起離開，留在這裡顯得安全多了，所以她就留下來等。

半鷹半獅的怪獸坐了起來，揉揉眼睛，看著皇后，直到她消失在視線外，才輕聲笑著說：「真是好笑！」他一半自言自語，一半對著愛麗絲說。

「有什麼好笑的？」愛麗絲問。

† Gryphon 是希臘神話中的怪獸，也是 Oxford 大學三一學院的徽章

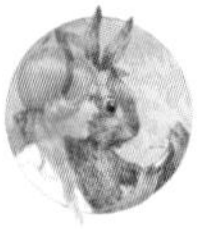

「那只不過是她的幻想罷了，她從沒處決過任何人！走吧！」怪獸說。

愛麗絲慢步跟在怪獸身後，心想：「這裡的人怎麼都喜歡說『走吧』？我這輩子還沒這樣被喚來喚去。」

還沒走遠，他們就看到前方的假烏龜孤獨傷心地坐在礁石上。當他們走近時，愛麗絲聽到假烏龜在嘆氣，很傷心的樣子。愛麗絲對牠深感同情，就問怪獸說：「牠在難過什麼？」怪獸用之前差不多的話回答說：「牠不過是愛胡思亂想，根本就沒什麼事好難過的。走吧！」

他們往假烏龜走去，假烏龜用含著淚水的大眼睛看著他們，一句話也沒說。

怪獸說：「這位小姑娘想聽你的故事。」

「我會告訴她的，請坐，在我講完之前，你們都不可以插嘴。」假烏龜的聲音又低又沉。

於是他們坐下來，安靜了片刻，愛麗絲心想：「故事沒有開頭，哪有講完的時候？」但她還是耐心等待。

終於，假烏龜深深地嘆了一口氣，說：「很久以前，我是一隻真烏龜。」

接著又是一陣久久的沉默，除了偶爾傳來怪獸的感嘆聲，再來就是夾雜著假烏龜持續的啜泣聲。愛麗絲差點就要站起來說：「先生，謝謝你的故事，實在是有趣極

了。」但是她又忍不住想，等一下一定就會有好玩的故事了，於是她靜靜地坐著，什麼也沒說。

最後假烏龜終於又開口了，語氣也比先前平靜，雖然偶爾還會有一、兩次啜泣聲，「小時候，我們到海裡上學，校長是一隻老烏龜——我們都叫牠陸龜——」

「你們為什麼叫牠陸龜？萬一牠不是陸龜呢？」愛麗絲問。

假烏龜生氣地說：「我們叫牠陸龜（Tortoise），是因為牠教我們東西（taught us），你真笨！」

「這麼簡單的問題都問得出來，你應該感到丟臉才對。」怪獸又添了一句。然後牠們倆就坐在那裡，一言不發地看著可憐的愛麗絲，愛麗絲恨不得有個地洞能鑽下去。最後，怪獸對假烏龜說：「繼續吧，老傢伙！別

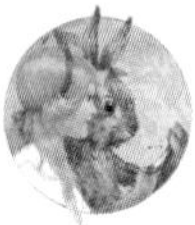

再拖了！」於是假烏龜便開始講他的故事。

「對，我們到海裡上學，這樣講你可能不信——」

「我沒有說我不相信！」愛麗絲打斷說。

「你就是有！」假烏龜說。

愛麗絲還沒來得及開口，怪獸就說：「閉上你的嘴！」於是假烏龜又繼續說下去。

「我們在那裡受到最好的教育——事實上，我們每天都得上學——」

愛麗絲說：「我們也是每天都要上學，這沒什麼好驕傲的。」

假烏龜急忙問道：「你們有額外的課程嗎？」

「有啊，我們還要學法文和音樂。」愛麗絲說。

假烏龜又問：「那洗衣呢？」

「當然沒有！」愛麗絲生氣地說。

假烏龜鬆了一口氣說：「噢，那你的學校不算是好學校，我們每年帳單的最後面都會有一條：『法文、音樂和洗衣——額外課程』。」

愛麗絲說：「你們不是住在海底嗎？不太需要學什麼洗衣啊。」

假烏龜嘆了一口氣說：「我付不起額外課程的費用，只修了一般的課程。」

「什麼是一般課程？」愛麗絲問。

假烏龜回答：「當然，剛開始是轉圈和翻騰†，然後是算數的分科——『野心』、『分心』、『醜容』和『嘲笑』†。」

† 轉圈（Reeling）和翻騰（Writhing）和 Reading 與 Writing 發音相近
† 四者和 Addition、Subtraction、Multiplication、Division 發音相近

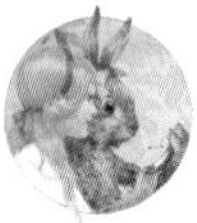

愛麗絲大膽地問：「我沒聽過什麼叫『醜容』，那是什麼啊？」

怪獸驚訝地舉起爪子，驚叫道：「什麼！你沒聽過醜容？我想你應該知道美容的意思吧？」

愛麗絲疑惑地說：「知道啊，就是讓東西——看起來——更漂亮。」

怪獸繼續說：「沒錯，如果你還不知道醜容是什麼，實在是有夠笨的！」

愛麗絲不敢再繼續問下去，只好轉向假烏龜問道：「除了這些，你還學什麼？」

假烏龜一邊數著手指，一邊回答說：「還有神祕學†，包括古典神祕學和現代神祕學，另外還有海洋學†和柔軟體操，教我們柔軟體操的老師是一隻老海鰻，牠一星期來上一次課，教我們把身體拉長、伸展和在線圈中昏倒†。」

「那是什麼樣的姿勢？」愛麗絲問

假烏龜說：「我現在沒有辦法表演給你看，因為我的身體已經太僵硬了，怪獸牠也沒學過。」

† 神祕學 Mystery 和 History 發音相近
† 海洋學 Seaography 和 Geography 發音相近
† 身體拉長、伸展和在線圈中昏倒：和 Drawing, Sketching and Painting in oil 取音相近

「我沒時間學，因為我去古典學老師那裡上課，牠是一隻老螃蟹。」怪獸說。

假烏龜嘆了一口氣說：「我沒上過牠的課，聽說他還開了『笑和悲傷』†的課程。」

「對啊，對啊！」怪獸說，輪到怪獸嘆氣了，然後兩人都把臉埋在爪子裡。

愛麗絲趕緊換話題說：「你們一天上課幾小時？」

假烏龜回答說：「第一天十小時，第二天九小時，以此類推。」

「好奇怪的課程！」愛麗絲大叫說。

怪獸說：「這也就是為什麼大家叫它「課程」（lesson）的原因了，因為上課的時間一天比一天少（lessen）。」

這種觀念對愛麗絲來說很新奇，她想了一會兒，便接著問說：「這樣第十一天就是假日囉？」

「當然。」假烏龜說。

「那第十二天怎麼辦？」愛麗絲熱切地追問。

「夠了，夠了，別再談課程了，現在跟她說說遊戲的事吧！」怪獸打斷話，堅決地說。

† 笑（Laughing）和悲傷（Grief）：和 Latin、Greek 發音相近

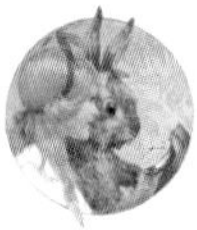

第十章

龍蝦的方塊舞

假烏龜又深深地嘆了一口氣，用一隻手遮住了眼睛，望著愛麗絲。牠想講話，卻好幾次哽咽得說不出話來。怪獸說：「你聲音聽起來好像骨頭卡到喉嚨似的。」然後就搖晃假烏龜的身體，並拍打牠的背。最後，假烏龜終於恢復正常的語調，兩行眼淚順著臉頰留下來，繼續說道：

「你沒住過很深的海底吧？」（愛麗絲回答說：「沒。」）「那你大概沒看過龍蝦囉？」（愛麗絲回答說：「我吃——」講到一半，便趕緊改口說：「沒，沒看過。」）「那你一定不知道龍蝦方塊舞有多好玩！」

愛麗絲說：「的確，我不知道，那是什麼舞啊？」

怪獸說：「就是先在海邊排成一列——」

假烏龜叫道：「應該是兩列才對！有海豹、烏龜等等，然後你要將所有的水母趕走——」

「這通常都需要一段時間，接著開始前進兩步——」怪獸插嘴說。

「每一步都要有龍蝦做舞伴。」怪獸叫道。

假烏龜說：「當然囉，前進兩步，和你的舞伴面對面——」

怪獸繼續說：「交換龍蝦舞伴，再恢復原來的隊伍。」

假烏龜接著說：「再來呢，就是拋出你的——」

「龍蝦舞伴！」怪獸大叫道，然後躍上了半空中。

「向海裡丟去，丟越遠越好——」

「隨著牠們向海裡游去！」怪獸尖叫說。

「在海裡翻一個觔斗！」假烏龜雀躍地蹦蹦跳跳。

怪獸喊叫說：「再交換一次舞伴！」

「回到岸上，不過那只是第一組舞步。」假烏龜的語調突然降下來說。原本像瘋子般跳來跳去的兩隻動物，突然悲傷安靜地坐下來，看著愛麗絲。

「這支舞跳起來一定很好看。」愛麗絲怯怯地說。

「你想看我們跳嗎？」假烏龜問道。

「當然想囉！」愛麗絲說。

假烏龜對怪獸說：「來！那我們來跳第一組舞步，雖然沒有

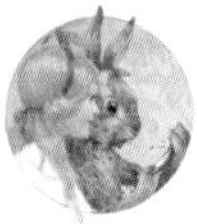

龍蝦，還是可以跳的。那誰來唱歌呢？」

「當然是你囉，我歌詞早忘光了。」怪獸說。

於是牠們圍著愛麗絲，正經八百地跳了起來，因為離得太近，還不時踩到愛麗絲的腳。牠們邊跳，還邊用前爪打拍子，假烏龜悲傷地緩緩唱著：

「鱈魚對蝸牛說：『你可以走快一點嗎？』
有隻海豚緊緊跟在我們後面，一直踩到我的尾巴。
看龍蝦和海龜跳得多盡興！
大家都在岸邊等——你願意跟我跳支舞嗎？
你願不願意、願不願意跟我跳支舞？
你願不願意、願不願意跟我跳支舞？

『你不知道，和龍蝦一起被舉起，
拋到海裡，多有趣啊！』
蝸牛斜著眼睛不悅地說：『太遠了！太遠了！』
牠客氣地回絕了鱈魚的邀請，不願和鱈魚共舞。
不想也不能，不想也不能，不願與鱈魚共舞。
不想也不能，不想也不能，不能與鱈魚共舞。

牠有鱗片的朋友問道：『被丟那麼遠有什麼關係？
海的另一邊也有岸，
你離英國越遠，就越接近法國。
親愛的蝸牛，別害怕，請與我跳支舞。

你願不願意、願不願意跟我跳支舞？
你願不願意、願不願意跟我跳支舞？」

「謝謝，這是一支好看有趣的舞。」愛麗絲很高興這一切終於結束了，「那首奇怪的鱈魚歌也很有趣。」

假烏龜說：「說到鱈魚，牠們——你應該看過吧？」

愛麗絲回答：「看過啊，我在餐——」愛麗絲發現自己又說錯話了，便趕緊住嘴。

假烏龜說：「我不知道『餐』是什麼地方，但如果你常常看到牠們，應該知道牠們長什麼樣子。」

愛麗絲想了一會兒說：「我想是的。牠們的尾巴都被塞在嘴裡，還有，牠們全身都撒滿了麵包粉。」

假烏龜說：「說到麵包粉，你好像講錯了，麵包粉在海裡會被沖掉。不過，牠們的尾巴倒是被塞在嘴裡，原因是——」說到這裡，假烏龜打了個哈欠，閉上眼睛，對怪獸說：「告訴她原因和事情的來龍去脈吧。」

怪獸說：「原因是牠們想和龍蝦跳舞，所以被丟到海裡，而且丟得很遠，所以很快就將尾巴緊緊塞在嘴裡。然後就無法把尾巴再從嘴裡拔出來了。就是這樣。」

「謝謝，這故事很有趣，我第一次聽到這麼多有關鱈魚的事。」愛麗絲說。

「如果你想聽的話，我還可以說更多，你知道鱈魚為什麼要叫做鱈魚（whiting）嗎？」怪獸說。

「這問題我沒想過，那是為什麼呢？」愛麗絲說。

怪獸認真回答：「因為牠們會擦靴子和鞋子。」

愛麗絲一頭霧水，好奇地重複問：「擦靴子和鞋子？」

「你不懂啊？你的鞋子是用什麼擦的？我的意思是，你是用什麼東西讓鞋子看起來這麼亮？」怪獸說。

愛麗絲低頭看了看自己的鞋子，想了一會兒說：「我想應該是用黑鞋油擦的。」

「在海底，我們的鞋子和靴子都是用白鞋油（whiting）擦的。現在你知道原因了吧。」怪獸繼續用低沉的聲音說。

愛麗絲更加好奇了，繼續追問說：「那你們的鞋子是用什麼做的？」

「當然是鰈魚和鰻魚，這種問題，連小蝦子都知道。」怪獸不耐煩地回答。

愛麗絲還在回想剛才那首歌，說：「如果我是鱈魚，我一定會跟海豚說：『拜託，離我遠一點，別老跟著我們！』」

假烏龜說：「牠們不得不讓海豚跟，只要是聰明的魚，如果沒有海豚的陪伴，牠們是哪兒也不會去的。」

「真的哪兒也不去嗎？」愛麗絲驚訝地說。

假烏龜說：「沒錯，如果有一隻魚來跟我說，牠要去旅行，我一定會問牠：『你要跟哪隻海豚（porpoise）一塊去？』」

「你應該是要問，你旅行的目的（purpose）吧？」愛麗絲說。

假烏龜生氣地說：「我說什麼就是什麼。」怪獸說了一句：「來，換我們來聽聽你的冒險故事。」

愛麗絲有些怯生生地說：「我可以告訴你們我今天早上到現在的冒險經歷，不過，至於昨天的就不行了，因為我已經是完全不同的人了。」

「請你解釋一下是什麼意思。」假烏龜說。

「不！不！先說冒險故事，解釋很花時間。」怪獸沒耐性地說。

於是，愛麗絲便從遇到白兔子開始，敘述她的經歷冒險。剛開始時愛麗絲有點緊張，假烏龜和怪獸分別坐在她的兩側，緊緊挨著她，聽得目瞪口呆，但越說就越不緊張了。兩位聽眾靜靜地坐著，直到愛麗絲敘述到背誦《威廉老爹》給毛毛蟲聽，所有的詞句都背錯時，假烏龜深深吸了一口氣說：「好奇怪。」

「怪得不能再怪了。」怪獸說。

「好像跟原來的句子完全不一樣！」假烏龜說。「這樣好了，現在就讓她背些東西來聽聽。叫她開始吧！」假烏龜看著怪獸，一副牠有權力對愛麗絲下命令的樣子。

「站起來，背那首《懶人之聲》看看。」怪獸說。

愛麗絲心想：「這些動物怎麼可以這樣隨便使喚別人，還叫我背誦！算了，就當作是在學校好了。」於是，她站起來背誦，可是她滿腦子都是剛才的龍蝦方塊舞，也不知道自己在背什麼，背出來的字句很奇怪：

這是龍蝦之聲，我親耳聽到牠說的，
『你把我烤得太黑，我得用糖刷我的頭髮。』
正如鴨子用眼皮，龍蝦用鼻子，
來調整皮帶、扣上釦子，還把腳趾頭往外扳。
等到沙子都乾了時，牠像雲雀一樣雀躍不已，
然後會用鯊魚的輕蔑語調說話；
不過等漲潮時，附近來了鯊魚，
牠講話的聲音就會很膽小，而且會發出打顫的聲音。

「這跟我們小時候背的好像不太一樣。」怪獸說。

假烏龜說：「我沒聽過這首歌，但聽起來的確是荒謬得離譜了些。」

愛麗絲一句話也沒說，只是把臉埋在手裡坐了下來，心裡想：難道事情不能恢復正常嗎？

「我希望你能解釋一下。」假烏龜說。

「她不能解釋，繼續背下一段。」怪獸急忙說。

假烏龜不理怪獸，繼續說：「可是你剛剛說到龍蝦的腳趾頭，牠怎麼可能用鼻子把腳趾頭往外扳呢？」

「那是第一種舞蹈姿勢。」愛麗絲說。但她的腦海已經一片混亂，很想換個話題。

怪獸又催促說：「請繼續下一段，再來是『我經過牠的花園』。」

愛麗絲知道再背下去還是會錯，但又不敢不從，只好顫抖著聲音背誦：

我經過牠的花園，一隻眼睛剛好看到
貓頭鷹和黑豹正在共吃一個派：
黑豹吃派的屑屑、肉汁和肉塊，
貓頭鷹吃著被招待的菜餚。
等派都吃完了，好心的給貓頭鷹湯匙
塞進口袋當謝禮：
而黑豹這時得到了刀和叉子，牠吼了一聲，
將這場盛宴做了個結束——

假烏龜打斷她的話說：「如果你一直說卻又不解釋，背這些東西要幹嘛？這是我聽過最難懂的事了！」

「對，我看你還是不要背了。」怪獸說，愛麗絲也巴不得趕快停下來。

怪獸繼續說：「你要不要再看我們跳另一首龍蝦方塊舞？還是你想要假烏龜唱一首歌給你聽？」

愛麗絲趕緊說：「唱歌好了，如果假烏龜願意的話。」怪獸不太高興地說：「哼！真是一點品味也沒有！老傢伙，再唱一首《烏龜湯》給她聽好了。」

假烏龜深深嘆了一口氣，開始唱著，並且不時帶著哽咽的聲音：

濃郁鮮美的湯，豐盛又翠綠，
盛在熱騰騰的湯盤裡。
如此的佳餚美饌，有誰不動心？
晚餐的湯，濃郁鮮美的湯！
晚餐的湯，濃郁鮮美的湯！
濃——郁鮮美的——湯！
濃——郁鮮美的——湯！
晚——餐的湯！
濃郁鮮美，濃郁鮮美的湯！

濃郁鮮美的湯！有誰還會在乎魚、遊戲
或其他的菜呢？
有誰能不為了這兩分錢的濃郁鮮美湯，
放棄所有一切呢？
值幾分錢的濃郁鮮美湯，
濃——郁鮮美的——湯！
濃——郁鮮美的——湯！
晚——餐的湯！
濃郁鮮美，濃郁鮮美的湯！

「又是副歌。」怪獸大叫，假烏龜正準備要開始重複時，遠處傳來一聲：「審判開始！」

「走吧！」怪獸大叫，拉著愛麗絲的手急忙地離開，等不及假烏龜把歌曲唱完。

「是誰要被審判？」愛麗絲邊跑邊喘氣問道，而怪獸只回答道：「走吧！」腳步卻更加快了，微風吹過，伴隨著越來越微弱的憂鬱歌聲：

晚——餐的湯！
濃郁鮮美，濃郁鮮美的湯！

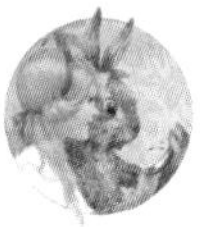

第十一章

誰偷了餡餅？

當他們抵達的時候，紅心國王和皇后坐在王位上，周圍有一群小動物和鳥圍繞著，還有一整副的撲克牌人也在那裡。侍者被五花大綁地押在他們面前，身旁各有一名士兵看守著。站在國王旁邊的是白兔，一手拿著小喇叭，另一手拿著一卷羊皮紙。法庭中央有一張桌子，上面擺了一大盤餡餅，看起來很好吃的樣子，愛麗絲看得都飢腸轆轆起來了。她心想：「真希望他們能趕快結束審判，然後發點心來吃！」但是照這種情況看來，好像不大可能，愛麗絲只好到處張望來消磨時間。

愛麗絲沒上過法院，不過她在書上讀過法院的事，她很高興，法庭上的每樣事物她大概都知道。她對自己說：「那應該就是法官了，他頭上戴了一頂大假髮。」

順便一提的是，那位法官就是國王，他把皇冠戴在假髮上（如果你想看國王怎麼戴假髮的話，請看插圖），看起來好像不怎麼舒服，事實上，這頂皇冠對他來講也太小了些。

This Style 10/6

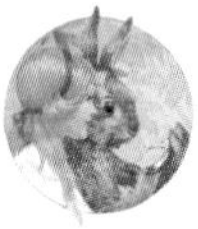

愛麗絲猜想：「這是陪審團的席位，而那十二隻生物（她不得不稱牠們為『生物』，因為有的是動物，有的是鳥類）應該就是陪審團員吧。」最後這個字，她驕傲地對自己重複了兩、三次，因為她認為，像她這樣年紀的女孩，沒幾個人懂得這些字的，而事實上也是如此。就算是陪審員，也不會懂的。

十二個陪審員都忙著在石板上寫字，愛麗絲悄悄地問怪獸：「牠們在寫什麼東西？為什麼審判還沒開始，牠們就開始寫東西了？」

怪獸小聲地回答：「牠們在簽名，怕等審判結束就會忘了名字。」

「笨蛋！」愛麗絲生氣地大聲說，不過，當白兔高聲喝道「法庭內保持肅靜」時，愛麗絲立刻把下面要說的話吞回去。而國王也戴上眼鏡，緊張地看著四周，看是誰在講話。

愛麗絲從陪審團員的背後可以看到，牠們都在石板上寫下「笨蛋」這兩個字；她甚至還知道，有一隻動物甚至連「笨蛋」這兩個字都不會寫，還問旁邊的人。愛麗絲心想：「審判還沒結束前，這塊石板就會被寫得亂七八糟了！」

有一位陪審員的筆在石板上嘎吱作響，愛麗絲無法忍受這種難聽的聲音，於是繞了法庭一圈，來到那位陪審員的後面，趁他不注意的時候，立刻把筆拿走。因為她的動作很快，那位可憐的陪審員（就是之前的蜥蜴比爾）根本不知道發生了什麼事，還探頭探腦地在找筆。由於實在找不到筆，所以接下來只好用手指頭寫，可是手指頭又不能在石板上留下字跡，因此寫了也是白寫。

「傳令官，將他的罪狀唸出來！」國王說。

聽到國王的命令，白兔馬上拿起小喇叭，吹奏了三聲，然後打開羊皮卷，開始唸：

炎炎夏日裡，
紅心皇后做了派，
紅心侍者偷了那些派，
偷走了所有的派！

「考慮好，給我你們的判決。」國王對陪審團說。

白兔急忙打斷國王的話說：「沒那麼快！還沒那麼快！在這之前還有很多程序！」

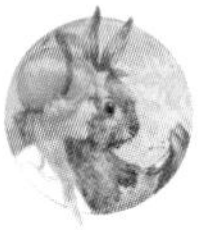

國王說：「傳喚第一位證人。」白兔於是吹了三聲小喇叭，大聲叫道：「傳第一位證人出庭。」

第一位證人是帽商，他走進來時，一手拿著茶杯，另一手拿著奶油麵包。說：「對不起，國王陛下，我不得不帶這些東西進來，因為我被傳喚時茶還沒喝完。」

國王說：「早該喝完了吧，你什麼時候開始喝的？」

帽商看了看跟隨他進入法庭的三月兔，手上還挽著睡鼠，便回答說：「我想應該是三月十四那天吧。」

「是十五日。」三月兔說。

「十六日才對。」睡鼠說。

「把這些記錄下來。」國王對陪審團說，陪審員於是趕緊將這三個日期寫在石板上，把它們加起來，再換算成先令與分。

「脫下你的帽子。」國王對帽商說。

「這不是我的。」帽商說。

國王對陪審團大叫：「偷竊罪！」陪審員立刻將這些話記錄下來。

帽商趕緊解釋道：「這些帽子是要賣的，我沒有自己的帽子，我是個帽商。」

聽到這裡，皇后便戴上了眼鏡，打量著帽商，帽商的臉色漸漸變得慘白而惴惴不安。

THIS STYLE
10/6
SILENCE
IN
THE

國王說：「把你所知道的證據都說出來，不要緊張，否則我就當場處決你。」

這句話不但沒有鼓勵他把證據說出來，反而讓他緊張得頻頻換腳站立，戰戰兢兢地看著皇后。在一陣慌亂中，竟把茶杯當成奶油麵包，咬了一大口。

就在此時，愛麗絲有一種奇怪的感覺，讓她感到很迷惑，後來她才發現自己又開始長大了。一開始，愛麗絲想要起身離開法庭，不過，想想反正這裡還有空間，於是又決定留在原地。

坐在愛麗絲旁邊的睡鼠說：「你不要一直擠過來好不好？我快要窒息了。」

「我也沒辦法，我正在長大。」愛麗絲溫和地說。

「你沒有權利在這裡長大。」睡鼠說。

愛麗絲大膽地說：「胡說八道，你也是會長大啊。」

睡鼠反駁說：「沒錯，可是我長大的速度很正常，沒像你這麼荒謬啊。」說完，便悻悻然地起身，走到法庭的另一邊去。

在這期間，皇后的視線都不曾離開過帽商，當睡鼠穿越法庭時，她突然對法警說：「把上次演唱會的歌手名單送上來！」可憐的帽商一聽，便開始發抖，抖得連兩隻鞋子都掉了。

國王生氣地重複說：「把知道的事實說出來，不然，不管你緊不緊張，我都要把你的頭砍了！」

帽商用顫抖的聲音說：「國王陛下，我只是個可憐的人，我喝茶——還不到一個星期呢——還有，我的奶油麵包越來越薄了——而我閃耀的茶——」

「閃耀的什麼？」國王說。

「就是以 tea 為首的字！」帽商說。

國王生氣地說：「我當然知道閃耀（twinkling）是 T 開頭，你當我是笨蛋！繼續說！」

帽商繼續說：「我只是個可憐的人，從那以後所有的東西都會閃耀，但那是三月兔說的——」

「我才沒有！」三月兔趕緊打斷他的話說。

「你有！」帽商說。

「我不承認！」三月兔說。

國王說：「牠否認，把這段刪掉。」

「那應該是睡鼠說的——」帽商一邊說，一邊緊張地看著睡鼠，怕牠也會否認，但睡鼠並沒有否認，因為牠已經睡著了。

帽商繼續說：「後來我多切了幾片奶油麵包——」

一位陪審員打斷他的話：「等一下，睡鼠到底說了什麼？」

「我不記得了。」帽商回答說。

「你一定要記得，不然就把你的頭砍了。」國王說。

可憐的帽商嚇得手上的茶杯和奶油麵包都掉到了地上，膝蓋不自主地跪了下去。他說道：「國王陛下，我只是個可憐的人。」

國王說：「你是個不會說話的人。」

這時有一隻天竺鼠突然發出歡呼聲，但馬上被法警壓制下來。（「壓制」這個字很難解釋，我把他們的動作告訴你：法警們拿了一個很大的帆布袋，把天竺鼠的頭裝進袋子裡，再用繩子把袋口綁好，然後坐在袋子上。）

愛麗絲心想：「真高興，我總算親眼看到什麼叫壓制了，我常在報紙上看到，在審判結束時，『總會有人

忍不住拍手叫好，但馬上就會被法警壓制下來。』可是我一直都不懂，現在我終於懂了。」

「如果你知道的只有這些，那你可以下去了（stand down）。」國王接著說。

帽商說：「可是，我不可能下去，我已經站在地上了。」

「好吧，那你坐下吧（sit down）。」國王回答說。

這時，又有一隻天竺鼠發出歡呼聲，立刻又被壓制下來。

愛麗絲心想：「哎，他們那樣收拾天竺鼠，實在應該要文明一點。」

「我想回去喝我的茶。」帽商說，還一邊緊張地看著皇后，而皇后正在看歌手的名單。

國王說：「你可以走了。」帽商連鞋子都還來不及穿，便急忙離開法庭。

皇后對身旁的法警說：「到外面把他的頭砍了。」法警還沒來得及趕到門口時，帽商已經消失無蹤。

「傳喚下一個證人！」國王說。

下一個證人是公爵夫人的廚師，她手裡還拿著一罐胡椒粉。甚至在她走進法庭之前，愛麗絲就已經立刻猜出是她了，因為靠門兩旁的人都在打噴嚏。

國王說：「把你所知道的事實都說出來。」

「我什麼都不知道。」廚師說。

國王不知所措地看著白兔，白兔低聲地提醒說：「國王陛下，您可以質詢這位證人。」

「好吧，如果一定要這樣做的話。」空氣瀰漫著一股低氣壓，國王皺起眉頭，看著廚子，眼睛簡直都快皺得看不到了，他雙手交叉於胸前，低聲說：「派到底是用什麼做的？」

「大部分是用胡椒做的。」廚師說。

廚師背後傳出剛睡醒的聲音：「是糖漿。」

皇后尖叫道：「抓住睡鼠，把牠頭砍下來！把牠趕出法庭！壓住牠！用力捏牠！把牠的鬍鬚一根根拔下來！」

突然間，法庭陷入一片混亂，等大家將睡鼠趕出去，再次就定位後，廚子就不見蹤影了。

國王鬆了一口氣，說：「沒關係！傳喚下一位證人。」接著便低聲地對皇后說：「親愛的，下一個證人由你來質詢，我的頭痛又犯了。」

愛麗絲好奇地看著白兔，笨拙地找名單，想知道下個證人會是誰。她對自己說：「因為他們根本就還沒有足夠的證據。」而出乎她意料之外的是，白兔竟高聲地喊著「愛麗絲」這個名字。

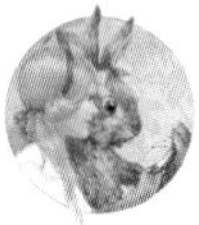

第十二章

愛麗絲的證詞

愛麗絲答了一聲：「有！」立刻站了起來，慌亂中忘了自己在幾分鐘前已經開始變得有多大了。結果裙子邊緣掃到陪審團，將陪審員掃到下面聽眾的頭上。大家七橫八豎地跌到了地上，讓愛麗絲想起上個星期不小心打翻的一缸金魚。

她驚慌地大叫：「喔，對不起！」然後盡快地抓起陪審員，因為她腦子裡還在想著打翻金魚缸的事，隱約地覺得如果不趕快把他們撿起來，放進陪審席裡，他們就會死掉。

國王嚴肅地說：「所有的陪審員趕快回到自己的位子上，不然審判就無法進行——」國王強調地說道，一邊睜大眼睛看著愛麗絲。

愛麗絲向陪審席看去，發現忙亂中把蜥蜴放顛倒了。可憐的小蜥蜴絕望地揮動著尾巴，動彈不得。愛麗絲趕緊把牠拔出來擺正，她自言自語說：「這沒什麼大

不了，不管牠是擺正還是顛倒，對這場審判也不會有太大的影響。」

等陪審員都恢復鎮定後，牠們的石板和鉛筆也都找到、遞回給牠們了。於是大家又開始努力地寫下剛才所發生的意外。除了蜥蜴以外，牠到現在還沒回過神，嘴巴張得開開的，傻傻地瞪著法庭的天花板。

國王問愛麗絲說：「這件事你知道多少？」

「完全不知道。」愛麗絲說。

「什麼都不知道？」國王繼續問。

愛麗絲說：「什麼都不知道。」

國王轉向陪審團說：「這很重要的。」當陪審團員正打算將這句話寫在石板上時，白兔插嘴說道：「國王陛下，您的意思是說這件事不重要。」白兔的語氣很恭敬，但牠邊說時，卻邊向國王擠眉弄眼的。

國王趕緊改口說：「當然，我的意思是不重要。」然後自己又低聲地說：「重要——不重要——不重要——重要——」好像在聽哪一個字比較好。

愛麗絲的位置很靠近陪審席，所以她可以看到有些陪審員在石板上寫下「重要」，有些寫下「不重要」。愛麗絲心想：「這一點都不重要，幹嘛寫這些？」

這時，正忙著在筆記本上寫東西的國王，喊了一聲：「肅靜！」接著將筆記本的條文唸了出來：「第四十二條規定，凡超過一哩高的人，必須退出法庭。」

於是每個人都看著愛麗絲。

「我沒有一哩高。」愛麗絲說。

國王說：「你有。」

「都快要兩哩了。」皇后加了一句。

愛麗絲說：「無論如何，我不走，況且根本就沒有這項規定，是你自己剛剛新加上去的。」

「這是筆記本裡最古老的規定。」國王說。

愛麗絲說：「如果是這樣，那應該是在第一條規定才對。」

國王臉色一陣青、一陣白，連忙闔上筆記本，用顫抖的聲音向陪審團說：「考慮一下你們的判決。」

白兔急得直跳腳，說：「國王陛下，還有很多證據，這是剛剛撿到的紙條。」

皇后說：「上面寫些什麼東西？」

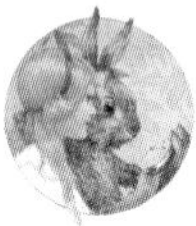

白兔說：「我還沒打開，不過看起來像是一封信，一封囚犯寫給某人的信。」

國王說：「這當然是一封信了，除非這個紙條不是寫給任何人的，但這種情形就不太正常了。」

「那封信是寫給誰的？」一名陪審員說。

「上面沒有指名要寫給誰，事實上，紙條外面什麼也沒寫。」白兔說，牠一邊打開紙條，一邊說：「沒錯，這不是一封信，這是一首詩。」

另一位陪審員問：「上面的字跡是囚犯寫的嗎？」

白兔說：「不是，不是，這件事真詭異。」（陪審團聽得一頭霧水。）

「那一定是模仿別人的字跡。」國王說。（所有的陪審員突然間又恍然大悟。）

侍者說：「國王陛下，不是我寫的，沒有人能證明這是我寫的，而且最後面也沒有簽名。」

「如果你沒有簽名，那只會讓事情更糟。你一定是心懷不軌，不然你會像個誠實的人一樣，在上面簽上你的名字。」國王說。

此時，現場響起了一片掌聲，因為這是國王到目前為止講過最有智慧的話了。

「這就證明了他有罪。」皇后說。

愛麗絲說：「這什麼也不能證明，而且你連紙條的內容是什麼都還不知道。」

「把它唸出來。」國王說。

白兔戴上了眼鏡，問道：「國王陛下，我該從哪裡開始唸？」

國王嚴肅地說：「從頭開始唸，唸到完就結束。」

於是白兔便開始唸下面的偈子：

他們說你去到過她那裡，
還在他的面前提到我，
她對我稱讚有加，
卻說我不會游泳。

他傳話給他們說，我沒去過那裡，
（我們都知道那是真的）
假如她想推卸責任，
你該怎麼辦？

我給她一塊，他們給他兩塊，
你又給我們三個或更多，

全部的東西又從他那裡回到你這裡來，
雖然以前它們是我的。

如果我或她
不小心捲入這事件，
他相信你可以讓他們自由，
正如我們從前所做的一樣。

就我所知，你曾是
（在她發瘋之前）
他、我們和它
之間的阻礙。

千萬別讓他知道，她最愛他們。
因為這是
你我之間的小祕密，
不能讓別人知道。

國王聽完後，摩拳擦掌說：「這是我們聽過最重要的證據，現在就讓陪審團——」

愛麗絲說：「如果有人可以解釋裡面的意思（過去幾分鐘內，愛麗絲又長大了許多，所以她一點也不怕打斷國王），我就給他六便士，我才不相信裡面會有什麼涵義。」

所有的陪審員都趕緊在石板上寫下：「她不相信這首偈子會有什麼涵義。」但卻沒有人要解釋這封信。

國王說：「如果這封首偈子沒有任何涵義，那就省了不少麻煩，因為我們不用費心去思索涵義了，不過，我還不確定。」他邊說，邊將偈子攤開在膝蓋上，用一隻眼睛端詳著，「我好像看出什麼端倪來了，『說我不會游泳——』你不會游泳，是吧？」國王轉向侍者問道。

侍者搖搖頭，傷心地說：「你看我像是會游泳的樣子嗎？」（它全身都是用厚紙板做的，當然不會游泳。）

國王說：「到目前為止都很好。」國王看著信，繼續喃喃自語地唸著那首偈子：「『我們都知道那是真的——』，這句當然是在描述陪審團——『我給她一塊，他們給他兩塊——』，這一定就是在指他在一起吃派的事了——」

愛麗絲說：「可是下一句接『全部的東西又從他那裡回到你這裡來——』」

國王勝利地指向桌上的派說：「不就擺在眼前了嗎？」國王對著皇后說：「事情再清楚也不過了，再來——『在她發瘋之前——』，親愛的，你好像沒有發瘋過吧？」

「當然沒有！」皇后一邊憤怒地說道，一邊拿起墨水台往蜥蜴砸過去。（可憐的小蜥蜴比爾，原本因為用手指無法在石板上寫出字來，已經停止寫字，這時竟急忙開始沾著墨汁寫了起來，也不管墨汁流了滿面。）

「這個字不適合[†]你。」國王說，微笑地環視著法庭，法庭上鴉雀無聲。

國王生氣地加了一句：「這是雙關語！」大家聽了哄堂大笑。

國王說：「讓陪審團投票表決。」這句話他至少已經講了二十次以上。

皇后說：「不行！不行！先處決再——表決。」

「這什麼話，哪有人先處決再表決的。」愛麗絲大聲抗議說。

皇后的臉色鐵青，說：「閉上你的嘴！」

「我不要！」愛麗絲頂了回去。

† fit 有「發瘋」和「適合」的不同意思

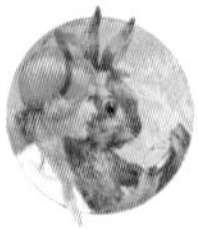

皇后氣得大叫：「把她的頭給砍下來！」可是卻沒有人敢動。

愛麗絲說：「誰怕你？（這時候愛麗絲已經恢復原來的大小了）你只不過是張撲克牌罷了。」

聽到這裡，所有的撲克牌突然都跳起來撲向愛麗絲，愛麗絲驚叫了一聲，又驚訝又生氣，想要揮開這些撲克牌。這時候，她發現自己躺在河岸邊，頭靠在姊姊的膝蓋上睡著了，而姊姊正輕柔地揮舞著從樹上掉下來的一些落葉，以免掉到她的臉上。

姊姊說：「親愛的愛麗絲，起來了！你睡得好甜啊！」

愛麗絲說：「我做了一個好奇怪的夢。」於是愛麗絲便將所記得的遊歷，統統告訴了姊姊，也就是你們剛才所讀的故事。等愛麗絲說完後，姊姊親了她一下，說：「這的確是個奇怪的夢！親愛的，但現在該去喝你的茶了，已經很晚了。」於是愛麗絲站起來，一路跑回家，還一邊想著，剛才的夢真奇怪。

當愛麗絲離開後，姊姊仍然坐在岸邊，用手撐著頭，看著落日的餘暉，回想著小愛麗絲剛才所說的奇遇冒險，想著想著，她也開始進入夢鄉，做起夢來了——

首先，她夢到小愛麗絲用小手緊緊地抱住膝蓋，睜著明亮的雙眼瞧著自己——她可以聽到愛麗絲每一個聲音，還有看到她特有的甩頭姿勢，將扎到眼睛的亂髮往後甩——就這樣聽著聲音，好像聽到妹妹夢中奇怪的動物，鮮活地出現在她四周圍。

白兔匆忙跑過，腳底下高高的草發出沙沙聲；在附近的水池中，膽顫心驚的老鼠潑著水，急著想要游到岸邊；三月兔和牠的朋友，正在享用著永無止境的茶會，她還可以聽到茶杯碰撞的聲音；而聲音尖銳的皇后正在處決倒楣的客人；公爵夫人膝上的小豬嬰兒，又打起了噴嚏，將杯盤在四周摔成了粉碎；半鷹半獅怪獸的尖叫怪聲、蜥蜴在石板寫字所發出的嘎吱聲，還有被壓在帆布袋裡天竺鼠所發出的呻吟，所有的聲音混雜著假烏龜遙遠的啜泣聲，瀰漫在空氣中。

姊姊坐了下來，閉上雙眼，想像自己身在夢幻仙境中，雖然她知道，只要睜開眼睛，所有的一切都會回到單調無聊的現實世界——草是因為風吹動才發出沙沙聲；蘆葦的搖動吹皺了一湖池水；茶杯碰撞的聲音，只不過是綿羊身上的鈴鐺；皇后的尖銳聲是牧童的叫喊聲；小嬰兒打噴嚏的聲音、怪獸所發出尖叫聲，還有其

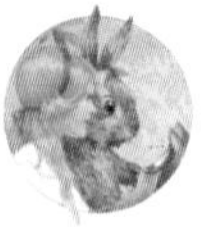

他各種奇怪的聲音，都將變成（她其實早就知道）忙碌農場上各種動物的喧鬧聲；遠處傳來母牛的哞哞聲，就是假烏龜的啜泣聲。

最後，姊姊在心裡想像著這個年幼的妹妹愛麗絲，日後終有一天會慢慢長大成一位成熟的婦人，但她自始至終一定會保持著童年的赤子之心。她會將小朋友們都叫到身邊來，跟他們說許許多多奇妙的故事，甚至可能會說這個年代久遠的夢遊仙境奇遇記，讓每個小孩都睜著好奇的大眼睛，聽得津津有味。她一定也能夠體會孩子單純的哀愁，還有在簡單的快樂中尋找樂趣的心情，她也一定會回想起，自己在夏日裡那段無憂無慮的童年時光。

作者 _ 路易士・卡洛爾
（Lewis Carroll）

譯者 _ 陳育堯
校對 _ 陳慧莉
封面設計 _ 蔡怡柔
製程管理 _ 宋建文

國家圖書館出版品預行編目資料

愛麗絲夢遊仙境（原著雙語彩圖本）(Alice's Adventures in Wonderland) / 路易士・卡洛爾（Lewis Carroll）著；陳育堯 譯. 一初版. 一[臺北市]：寂天文化, 2013.4 面； 公分.

ISBN 978-986-318-093-7 (25K平裝)

873.59 102004972

出版者 _ 寂天文化事業股份有限公司
電話 _ +886-2-2365-9739
傳真 _ +886-2-2365-9835
網址 _ www.icosmos.com.tw
讀者服務 _ onlineservice@icosmos.com.tw
出版日期 _ 2015年5月 初版再刷（250102）
郵撥帳號 _ 1998620-0 寂天文化事業股份有限公司
訂購金額600（含）元以上郵資免費
訂購金額600元以下者，請外加郵資65元
若有破損，請寄回更換